"People c   ood
or bad. Life is   stin,
Melissa's mot

"The rai   ist?"
Jory asked.

"Yes, but regardless, we still have one very real thing going for us. We have 'hope,' and I think that's what separates us from the rest of creation. We get to hold on to hope . . . hope for things not seen."

Jory was moved by Mrs. Austin's faith, and she wondered if she'd ever feel that way herself. Would she ever come to accept gracefully what she couldn't understand or change?

Other Bantam Books you will enjoy

STARRY, STARRY NIGHT by Lurlene McDaniel
TOO YOUNG TO DIE by Lurlene McDaniel
PLEASE DON'T DIE by Lurlene McDaniel
DON'T DIE, MY LOVE by Lurlene McDaniel
ALL THE DAYS OF HER LIFE
   by Lurlene McDaniel
BABY ALICIA IS DYING by Lurlene McDaniel
TIME TO LET GO by Lurlene McDaniel
A FAMILY APART by Joan Lowery Nixon
THE YEAR WITHOUT MICHAEL
   by Susan Beth Pfeffer

GOODBYE DOESN'T MEAN FOREVER

Lurlene McDaniel

BANTAM BOOKS

NEW YORK · TORONTO · LONDON · SYDNEY · AUCKLAND

RL 4, IL age 10 and up

GOODBYE DOESN'T MEAN FOREVER
A Bantam Book / August 1989

ISBN 0-553-28007-4

Published simultaneously in the United States and Canada

Bantam Books are published by Bantam Books, a division of Bantam
Doubleday Dell Publishing Group, Inc. Its trademark, consisting of the
words "Bantam Books" and the portrayal of a rooster, is Registered in U.S.
Patent and Trademark Office and in other countries. Marca Registrada.
Bantam Books, 1540 Broadway, New York, New York 10036.

PRINTED IN THE UNITED STATES OF AMERICA

20   19   18   17   16   15   14

For Rochelle

"Now faith is the substance of things hoped for, the evidence of things not seen."

HEBREWS 11:1 (KJV)

GOODBYE DOESN'T MEAN FOREVER

Chapter One

"Jory Delaney, you can't be serious! What do you mean you don't want to go to Europe with your father and me next month?"

"Mother, please, give me a break. School starts at the end of August. You won't be back by then and I can't miss the start of my senior year. Besides, I don't feel like exploring ruins and visiting a bunch of moldy castles." Jory faced her mother across the glass-topped table on their patio next to the pool. Her breakfast lay cold and untouched, and butter melted in a crystal dish in the rapidly warming Florida morning.

"Well, that's the silliest thing I've ever heard." Mrs. Delaney tossed her pink linen napkin onto the colored flagstones and pushed her chair backward, making it screech. "You have the opportunity of a lifetime here, and you're throwing it away. Missing your first week of school can't be that big a deal."

"Well, it is to me."

Mrs. Delaney dismissed Jory's words with a flip of her hand. "Your father and I work very hard. This is the first non-working vacation we've planned in years and you don't want to go. That is such an insult."

1

Jory gritted her teeth, biting back the hot words she longed to throw at her elegant blond mother. *Sure, mother,* she thought sarcastically. *Just a cozy little family threesome.* After all the years they'd shuttled off on their real estate deals, leaving Jory under the care of some anonymous housekeeper, now they wanted her to drop everything and take off with them.

"You and Daddy go to Europe, Mother. I'll be perfectly happy to stay here and start school on time. And I'm sure Mrs. Garcia will see to it that I don't starve to death." She emphasized her retort with a toss of auburn curls.

"Well, don't worry. We will." Mrs. Delaney said coolly.

"Fine. Then it's settled."

Silence hung between mother and daughter. The bright blue water of the pool sparkled with the sun. On the far side of the patio a sprinkler spun, tossing water over boxwood and summer flowers. "Jory, your refusal really burns me up. You won't be but a week late in starting school if you come with us. What's a week compared to a monthlong tour of Europe?"

It wasn't over. "I told you," Jory said with an exasperated sigh. "Europe and old castles and quaint cottages aren't my idea of a good time."

"And just what is? Going to public high school with a bunch of riffraff? Honestly, Jory, we'd send you to Tampa's best private school if you'd say the word. And Briarwood School for Young Women doesn't start classes until after Labor Day, so that

would you give you plenty of time to get home before school begins if that's what's stopping you from
coming."

"The word is no, Mother. I *like* Lincoln High."
She stabbed a strawberry from a selection of fresh
fruit arranged on a crystal platter. She didn't want
her mother to dredge up that old argument about
Jory's choice of public over private school.

"Your father and I have worked very hard for all
this." Mrs. Delaney gestured around the patio and
yard, which were carefully secluded behind an
eight-foot security fence. "Money is security,
Jory—not a curse. You certainly have enjoyed its
benefits so far. A new convertible, the latest fash-
ions, a home in the most exclusive area of
Tampa . . ."

Unable to stand her mother's count-your-bless-
ings-speech one more time, Jory jumped up. "I'm
going for a swim." She tugged at the French-cut leg
of the green suit that hugged her body like a latex
glove.

"It's that Austin girl, isn't it?" Her mother's ac-
cusatory tone caused Jory to stop short. "Ever since
she came down with cancer last year, that's all
you've been concerned about."

Jory suddenly became calm and said, "Melissa
Austin is my best friend and has been since the fifth
grade. And yes, I'm concerned about her. Even
though her leukemia is in remission, she isn't
cured. She's the bravest person I've ever known."
Jory wanted to say more. She wanted to remind her
mother that it was Melissa who opened her home to

Jory over the years when her own parents had been too busy earning money to be available. In some ways, Jory even thought of Mrs. Austin as her second mother.

Mrs. Delaney arched one perfectly shaped eyebrow and tapped long manicured red fingernails against the glass tabletop. "Loyalty is an admirable quality," she said, "but there's more at stake here than old friends and returning to high school on time, isn't there? Face it, Jory, you aren't exactly headed toward scholastic immortality in your schoolwork. Have you followed up on any of those college applications your father wanted you to?"

"No."

"And why not? Most of your friends have already finished their applications and you haven't even started. Once you graduate next June, just what do you plan to do with yourself?"

Jory tipped her chin, her green eyes as cool and hard as her mother's diamond rings. "Maybe I'll run off with the gardener and get married."

"That's not funny, Jory. You have money—lots of it in a trust fund. You're seventeen and without purpose or direction. If you won't choose a college and you refuse to go to Europe this summer, what are you going to do? We won't have you sitting around when there's so much at stake in your future."

Jory was so angry she was shaking, but she knew that she couldn't speak rationally. Her mother rose in one fluid motion, her floor-length silk lounging robe billowing around her. "That was an unnecessary and tacky comment about marrying the gardener. Use some discretion. Don't make people gossip. We have an image to maintain in Tampa, you know."

"I'll keep your request in mind," Jory said through pressed, white lips. "We don't want people to talk about your shiftless daughter, do we?"

"Don't be so melodramatic. Reputations are important, and what you do now can follow you the rest of your life." Mrs. Delaney glanced at her gold watch. "I have to dress and meet your father at the club. We're entertaining some Arab businessman who's interested in one of the old estates on Bayshore Drive. It'll mean a tidy commission if we close the deal. But don't think this conversation is ended, Jory. I'll let you stay home from Europe this trip, but I expect you to do something about your future. And you'd better get started. Time's running out for you to get into a good college."

Jory swore she saw dollar signs flash in her mother's eyes before she swept through the patio's French doors, leading into the house. Still trembling, Jory plunged into the cool blue water of the pool, balling her body to stay weighted on the concrete bottom.

Beneath the surface, it was quiet, serene. She opened her eyes, allowing the chlorine to sting and take the place of angry tears. Jory wasn't stupid. She knew that her wealth gave her a cushion. She thought again of Melissa, of the horrible cancer that lurked within her body. She thought of the chemo that had stripped her of her hair and her beauty.

Jory also knew her mother was right. Life had smiled on Jory Delaney. For years, she'd dated and partied and lived exactly as she pleased. But there was a void inside her too. In some ways, Melissa had so much more than she did, in spite of her cancer.

Lungs bursting, Jory struggled to the surface, gasping for air. She swam to the side and heaved herself onto the glazed tile border. "Well, Mother, thanks to me at least she's pretty again," she muttered, remembering with satisfaction the waist-length wig she'd given Melissa as a gift. She stretched backward onto the tile, allowing the sun to warm her golden skin. And as for her mother's warning about who to date . . .

For Jory, there was only Michael Austin, Melissa's dark-haired, blue-eyed, brother. He was twenty-two but seemed older. For as long as Jory had known the Austins, Michael had been son and brother and father. When Mr. Austin walked out on his family, Michael stepped into his role while their mother worked. Now, between his jobs and classes at the university and an occasional ride in his hot-air balloon, Michael seemed to have no other life. Jory longed to change that. She could be so much to him if only he'd let her.

"Michael . . ." She whispered his name. He'd always thought of her as Melissa's spoiled rich friend, a kid, but she'd prove him wrong. She recalled the one time when he hadn't looked at her like she was a child, the night last spring when she'd given Melissa the wig.

"You did this for Melissa?"

"Why not? What are friends for?"

His hand drifted up to stroke her cheek. She gazed at him through thick lashes, her heartbeat fluttering and erratic. "Thank you." He tipped her chin upward and lightly brushed her bangs off her forehead before trailing his fingers over the arch of her cheekbone.

She could have drowned in his eyes. She almost lost emotional control and whispered, "I love you, Michael . . ."

Restless, tingling with the memory, Jory sat up. She would dress and drive over to Melissa's. With school starting in five weeks, they could talk about new wardrobes and what it would be like to be seniors and speculate whether Melissa would be named a National Merit semifinalist. And maybe, if she was very lucky, she'd catch a glimpse of Michael.

"Hey, Jory. How goes it?" Melissa asked as Jory coasted into her friend's driveway.

"Okay. How goes it with you?" Jory climbed over the side of her convertible and walked to the kitchen door, where Melissa waited behind the screen. Melissa was wearing not her waist-length hairpiece but, instead, her own hair, regrown into a sleek black cap.

"They make doors for cars, you know."

"A nuisance." She followed Melissa to the kitchen counter, strewn with the makings for soup and pasta salad. "What are you doing?"

"I thought I'd get a head start on dinner for Mom. She's training a new group of operators at the phone company today and that sort of thing always wears her out."

Jory felt totally comfortable in the familiar Austin house. Her eyes darted from the worn wallpaper to the refrigerator, cluttered with notes and magnets, to the old pine table where she'd shared so many meals with Melissa, Mrs. Austin, and Michael. "Smells yummy," she said, popping a chunk of chicken into her mouth.

"Didn't you have breakfast?"

"Lost my appetite," Jory said, unable to keep the sarcasm out of her voice.

"What happened?"

Jory shrugged, deciding not to mention Europe. "I had a tiny run-in with Mother. She and Dad keep fussing about my going to a private school." Jory silently wished that her mother were more like Melissa's. Mrs. Austin always seemed to have time for her family, in spite of how long and hard she worked. Jory never heard her griping at Melissa about how to live *her* life.

"A private school's name on your diploma would make any college look harder at you," Melissa said, chopping celery.

Jory knew she could never make Melissa understand that an exclusive college campus wouldn't make the idea of four more years of school any more attractive to her. The fact was that while she was innately smart, she loathed disciplined study habits. "I know I've got to decide something soon about my future. But right now, life's too short and the summer's almost gone."

Life's too short. Jory could have bitten her tongue for using that particular phrase. But if her friend noticed, she didn't let on. "You sound like Scarlett O'Hara—'I'll think about it tomorrow.'"

"Oh fiddley-dee," Jory said with a flap of her lashes.

"I saw Brad last week," Melissa said casually.

"Oh, yeah? How's the former captain of our victorious Brain Bowl team doing?"

"Getting ready to head for Yale. And it was an *almost* victorious Brain Bowl team," Melissa corrected, punctuating the air with the tip of her paring knife. "We lost in the state finals, and you know it."

"Wasn't your fault," Jory griped. "The judges were prejudiced toward the Miami team."

"We'll get them next time. Don't forget, I'm going to be captain when Lincoln selects its new team next spring."

Jory grinned. "I thought you had to try out for the panel. Or does rank have privilege because you're one of the few returning players from last year?"

"Lyle Vargas will be back. You remember him?"

Jory puckered her brow. "A science whiz, right? He makes me yawn."

"Really? He speaks highly of you, you know."

"Definitely not my type. Give me dark, handsome, and older anytime."

"What's all the noise out here?" Jory felt her
heart pound at the sound of the voice. She turned
from the counter to see Michael, rumpled and disheveled and unbearably sexy, standing in the doorway. She smiled at him, but his blue eyes swept
past her as if she weren't there.

Chapter Two

"Well, good morning," Melissa said. "What woke you from your long summer's nap?"

"The smell of food and female chatter," Michael rumbled, sticking his head into the open refrigerator.

When he reemerged Jory shifted, trying not to feel hurt. She eyed him covetously. His upper body was bare, tight with tanned muscles from working in the sun. Well-worn jeans hugged his lean hips.

Michael clutched a carton of milk and a small bag of powdered-sugar donuts and wandered to the table. "I worked construction until three yesterday, then took the late shift at the grocery warehouse. I've had four hours of sleep and I chew up little girls who stand around in the kitchen giggling." He opened the carton of milk and downed a swig.

Melissa brandished her paring knife. "Careful, or I'll cut off your ears."

"Watch it, Melissa, he really does look mean," Jory interjected, propping her elbows on the counter. She decided to act flip, desperate to be more to him than a "little girl."

"Can't you two go wander around the mall or something? I need my sleep."

11

"We'll be out of here as soon as I finish making dinner."

"Do you want to hit the mall?" Jory asked, in no hurry to be away from Michael.

Melissa dropped her gaze. "I can't. I've got a clinic appointment at noon."

Jory saw the muscles work in Michael's jaw while she felt a sinking sensation in the pit of her stomach. Wouldn't her best friend's life ever be normal again? Michael asked, "How are you getting there? Why didn't you work out something with Mom? I can hitch a ride to work if you want to borrow my pickup."

"Mom had a hard day ahead of her and I didn't want to complicate it. It's no big deal, Michael. I go to the clinic twice a month, you know. I'll just take the bus," Melissa said brightly.

"Like hell," Michael snapped. "You got sick last time and almost didn't make it back."

Melissa blushed, obviously embarrassed. "Don't be silly," Jory interrupted hastily. "I've got nothing to do today. I'll take you."

"Oh, Jory, it's a long visit today. They're doing a lumbar puncture, and if I don't lie perfectly still for at least half an hour afterward, I get the world's worst headache. There's nothing for you to do but sit and wait."

"I don't care. I'll read."

"You hate to sit and read."

"Let Jory take you." Michael's command settled the matter instantly. He stretched out in his chair, his long legs crossed at the ankles, and ate donuts. Jory made a stab at starting a conversation, but the good humor of the day had evaporated. Melissa finished quickly in the kitchen, and after she changed Jory drove her to the clinic.

"Keep the top down," Melissa said when Jory started to raise the soft cloth roof of her car.

"But I thought the sun was bad for you."

"Some of my medications react to too much sun, but I doubt I'll turn splotchy in a twenty-minute ride." Melissa's tone was cynical. Jory watched her friend from the corner of her eye as Melissa rested her head on the bright red upholstery and turned her face toward the sunlight. "I'll bet I'm the only girl at Lincoln who returns this year without a tan," she grumbled. "God, I miss going to the beach."

Jory missed going with her. They hadn't been once all summer. "The beach is hot and sticky anyway," Jory said. "Who needs it?"

"*I* need it." Melissa sighed. "It's the ocean I really miss. And the waves."

"And the good-looking guys," Jory joked, in an effort to chase away Melissa's doldrums.

"Aren't I allowed even a small pity party?"

"Absolutely not. You don't see me feeling sorry for myself because your brother acts like I'm part of your household fixtures, do you?" She shook her head as she parked in the clinic lot. "No-o-o. Not Jory Delaney. She just picks her tongue up off the floor every time she's around Michael and keeps on smiling." Jory's speaking about herself in the third person made Melissa chuckle. She couldn't stand seeing Melissa down-and-out. "And incidentally, I'm going to have to get tough with Michael if he's not careful."

"Tough?"

"I'm just going to have to grab him, throw him to the floor, and ravish him. Not that I'm a pushy broad, but I'm tired of waiting for him to ravish me. Lord knows I've been waiting since the sixth grade!"

They entered the clinic, laughing. Melissa signed in and Jory found a seat, moving some toys left by the younger kids. She glanced around the building and shuddered. The place gave her the willies. The smells, the sounds, the sight of so many kids with cancer caused her nerves endings to itch. How did Melissa stand it?

As soon as Melissa was called into the lab area, Jory went outside for fresh air. The July heat was oppressive. In another month school would start. *My senior year,* she thought. She'd be a graduate by the following June. Jory wished she cared.

She would, however, have to think of something to get her mother off her back so that she could enjoy her final year of high school. She glanced toward the beige brick of the hospital and thought about Melissa getting needles poked into her veins and her spine. Jory wished there were something she could do for her friend. *Something* that would make the pain go away and make their senior year memorable.

* * *

"Are you going to be all right?" Jory couldn't conceal her terror. They sat in the blazing sun on the shoulder of the road while Melissa leaned out the open door and vomited. Jory felt helpless, panicked, as she patted Melissa's sweat-drenched back and tried to comfort her friend.

"I'll . . . be . . . fine." Melissa managed between gags.

"This is the pits!" Jory said, raising the convertible's roof. She turned on the air-conditioning full blast to ward off the unbearable heat. Her blouse stuck to her skin. She'd helped Melissa before, but she'd been in the hospital then and there had been nurses close by. Now, Jory knew, there was no one but herself. "I think the cooler air will help," she told Melissa above the roar of the air conditioner fan. *Be all right, Melissa. Please, be all right*, she prayed silently.

Slowly, the heaving subsided and Melissa sagged against the car seat, her face pinched and white. Gently, Jory reached across, closed the car door, and stroked Melissa's clammy forehead. Melissa's eyelids fluttered open. "Sorry about that." Her voice sounded raw and small.

"What's the big deal? You think I've never puked before? Remember that time I had the flu? You were there for me."

"True . . . we've certainly made some lasting memories." Melissa made a stab at humor.

Jory threw the car into drive, checked for oncoming traffic, and lurched the car off the shoulder and onto the road. Gravel spat from under the tires. "Do you feel better?"

Melissa eased upright and nodded. "Yes. Can we stop for a cold drink?"

"There's a mini-mart up ahead. I'll get us a couple of sodas."

After they were back on the road Melissa asked, "Where are we?"

"Just driving around. There's not much traffic out this way, and I thought you might not want to go home right now."

"You're right." Melissa gazed out at her surroundings. "Wait a minute."

"What is it?" Jory grew anxious, afraid that Melissa would be sick again.

"I've been on this road before. There's a place off a dirt road . . . Ric brought me. There!" She pointed. "Turn here."

Jory followed Melissa's directions and maneuvered her car down a twisting dirt lane, draped with drooping tree branches. When she reached a small clearing, she turned off the engine and they sat in the summer quiet. A stream gurgled over rocks nearby. "Not bad," she said.

"Put the top down. I need some fresh air."

Overhead, Spanish moss hung from trees, and they could hear insects chirping. "Ric brought you here?"

"Yes, last spring. It's sort of peaceful, don't you think?"

"Sure do." Jory sipped her soda. "What happened when he brought you?"

Mischief sparkled in Melissa's blue eyes, letting Jory know that she was feeling better. "He asked to make love to me."

Jory's jaw dropped. "Really? What did you say?"

"I told him I'd think about it."

"And?"

"And I thought about it."

Exasperated, Jory squealed, "Don't do this to me, Melissa Austin! What did you *do*?"

"I told him no. It wasn't right for me."

"I don't know what I'd say if someone I really cared about asked me," Jory confessed, thinking of Michael. But then, he'd never ask her.

Melissa swirled the cola can, and Jory listened to the liquid slosh. "So who's asked you who you *didn't* really care about?"

"Are you kidding? I've been slapping guys' hands away since eighth grade. Honestly, a girl gets a reputation for parties and good times, and guys think they can get away with anything."

"Don't tell me you're giving up the party life this school year?"

"Maybe. My mother wants me to 'get serious' about my future."

"What's that mean?"

"To my mother, it's being seen in the right places with the right people."

"A party's a party," Melissa observed. It bothered Jory that everyone, even Melissa, had this image of her as frivolous and shallow. No wonder Michael thought of her as a silly kid.

"Don't bet on it. I like to pick my parties and my friends. Mother thinks that the masses at Lincoln aren't good enough for me. Or rather for our family's position in Tampa."

"Sorry. I didn't mean it like it sounded. You know I think you're terrific." Melissa plucked at lint on the upholstery. "I can't wait for school to start because it puts me that much closer to college. That much closer to law school and a career."

Jory felt pangs of envy. Melissa knew exactly what she wanted—if she could live long enough to achieve it. Jory didn't know anything she wanted—and she'd probably live forever. She sighed, starting the car.

"Michael's taking his balloon up this Saturday at dawn," Melissa said. "Why don't you come with me and help him launch it like we did last summer?" Jory's pulse automatically accelerated and Melissa continued, tenderly, "Who knows? Maybe this time he'll take you up with him."

"Who knows?" Jory echoed, feeling her spirits soar. *To touch the sky with Michael* . . . Well, perhaps she could think of *one* thing she wanted.

Chapter Three

～

Jory shivered in the damp fog. Members of Michael's hot-air balloon club scrambled to unfurl their nylon ships and launch them before the sun could rise. She nudged Melissa, asking, "Why's Michael late? Will the fog keep him from going up?" Melissa had spent the night at Jory's house, and the two of them had arrived at the field first.

"He said he'd meet us here," Melissa said. "And this fog's nothing. The sun will burn it right off. Besides, it's a low fog and the balloons will be above it in minutes."

Jory listened to the hiss of the propane tanks. She watched a balloon fill and rise like a colorful soap bubble. Once filled with heated air, the balloon strained against ropes as a ground crew held it to the earth and two people climbed into a gondola-shaped basket. Light from the headlamps of parked vans and trucks tunneled through the fog, making the seven-story-tall balloon seem like a ghostly galleon for aliens. "My hands are sweating," she confessed to Melissa in a whisper.

"Why?"

"Because I might get to go up in Michael's balloon with him."

"Now that wasn't a firm promise," Melissa warned. "I said *maybe*."

"'Maybe' was all it took for me to crawl out of bed at four A.M. and drive out here with you, wasn't it?"

"If you do go up, don't get sick like I always do. My stomach is definitely a landlubber."

"That's sailor talk—not ballooning," Jory said with a grin.

"Nausea knows no distinction," Melissa said, holding her palm against her abdomen.

Jory watched as another balloon rose, its pilot adjusting the smaller propane burner aboard his craft. The bright flame shot upward into the neck of the balloon. "You're sure the fabric won't catch on fire?" she asked, feeling apprehensive for the first time.

"Michael says that's what keeps them up in the sky. When a pilot wants his balloon to go higher, he turns up the burner. If he wants to go lower, he lets the air inside the balloon cool naturally, or he releases it through a special valve." Melissa punctuated her explanation with her hands as she talked. "It's tricky though, because it takes time for the balloon to respond. That's why these people have a pilot's license."

Surprised, Jory interrupted. "I didn't know Michael had a license to fly."

"It's the law. And there has to be a chase crew—like us—on the ground," Melissa continued. "In case a pilot gets into trouble with power lines or something."

"The things I do for love . . ." Jory mumbled.

"Here he comes."Melissa pointed to a pickup approaching over the bumpy terrain. The truck skidded to a halt and Michael jumped out and hurried to lower the tailgate.

"Oversleep, Big Brother?" Melissa needled.

"Beth overslept," he corrected, his hands busy hauling out the massive nylon balloon from his truck bed.

"Beth?" Jory asked blankly in unison with Melissa. Then for the first time, she noticed the passenger inside the truck. A girl, blond and still sleepy-eyed, pushed the creaky door open and stepped to the ground. She smiled sheepishly. "Beth Collins. Are you Melissa?"

"Beth's in my macroeconomics class at USF," Michael explained as he worked to lay the balloon out on the ground. "I promised to take her up this morning."

Jory felt twinges of hurt and jealousy. She exchanged glances with Melissa, who stepped toward Michael. "I thought Jory might go up with you."

"Sorry, my basket can only hold two. Here, hold this rope while I drag the propane tank over."

Jory shuffled out of the way, numb and embarrassed. *Stupid*, she told herself. How stupid of her to ever think she had a chance with Michael.

"Can I help?" Beth asked.

"Hold the other rope," Michael directed, aiming the nozzle of the tank at the mouth of the balloon. He turned the valve, the tank hissed, and the yellow-and-red material fluttered and began to fill.

"How'd you get into hot-air ballooning?" Beth asked, her face pretty and attentive in the growing morning light. "I heard balloons like this are expensive."

"I accepted it as a payoff on a bad debt that some guy owed me. I worked a whole summer and the guy's construction company went bankrupt. He gave me the balloon to keep me from blowing his head off." Michael grinned. Jory tried to ignore the way his nearness made her insides turn to jelly. He talked as he worked. "And yes, it is expensive. But it's my only vice."

By now, the balloon had filled, and its bright panels of fabric stretched and reached toward the sky. "It's beautiful," Beth shouted, holding fast to the rope.

"Come on. Get in the basket before we miss what's left of the sunrise."

With envy, Jory watched Beth scramble into the wicker gondola, followed by Michael. "Toss off the ropes," he commanded Melissa and others who'd gathered to help with the launch. Michael released a blast of propane from the tank on board the balloon, and the great airship rose. "Hey," he called down to Melissa. "You two will be my spotters won't you? You and Jory follow in my pickup, and after we land I'll treat everybody to breakfast."

"Jory and I'll follow," Melissa shouted.

The balloon floated up, and as it climbed Jory felt her fantasies floating away with it.

"I'm sorry." Melissa's voice interrupted her thoughts.

Jory turned and forced a smile. "What's the big deal? You told me all along that it was chancy that he'd take me with him."

"I didn't know a thing about this Beth."

"Well, aren't you always saying he needs more of a social life and I need to concentrate on guys my own age?"

"Yes, but . . ."

"Then that's just what I'm going to do." Jory got inside the truck and slammed the door a little too hard. "After all, school starts in a few weeks and there's a whole army of senior guys waiting to be conquered." Suddenly, she half wished she'd gone to Europe with her parents.

"That's the spirit," Melissa said, sliding behind the wheel and starting the engine. "We'll come back for your car later," she added, putting the truck into gear and heading across the field.

Jory gritted her teeth as the vehicle bumped along, forced down a lump of bitter disappointment, and scanned the sky. The fog had evaporated and dawn had broken out in shades of pink and violet. The balloon floated on a hazy draft of warm summer air. She watched it recede, carrying her hopeless love for Michael along with it.

"You're awfully quiet, Jory. And you didn't eat much at breakfast. Was it because of Beth?"

Melissa's question stirred Jory long enough for her to adjust her rearview mirror and realize that she'd passed her exit on the expressway. "It was gruesome," she confessed. "I didn't like sitting there watching Beth make nice-nice with him. But it's more than that."

"Like what?"

Jory shrugged, not sure she was able to verbalize her churning thoughts. "I feel like Rip van Winkle. I woke up one day and discovered that life had passed me by and all I was was older."

"I don't get it."

"You have all these dreams and plans, Melissa. I don't have anything. No goals. No stars to shoot for." She released a short, derisive laugh. "Do you know how awful it makes me feel to admit my mother's right?"

"Geez, Jory, you're seventeen. You've got a million years to make plans."

Jory glanced toward her friend. "That's what *I've* been telling *you* for years. But you kept telling me that life was more than one long party. That I needed to think about my future and college."

Melissa flushed. "I'm not contradicting myself. You do need to think about those things. I guess I hate to see you down, that's all. And all because Michael showed up this morning with a girl."

"It just made me realize how I get focused on one thing and forget about everything else."

"That's not true. You're just loyal."

"I'm a dope," Jory corrected.

"Well when school starts, something or someone will come along and make you happy again."

Jory saw Melissa's hand resting against the seat. It was thin and pale, and it reminded Jory of her best friend's battle against cancer. Again, the unfairness of life smacked her conscience. "So help me dedicate this year to 'finding myself.' Okay?"

Melissa poked Jory's shoulder. "Only if you smile and tell me you haven't given up on Michael."

"But you're *always* after me to give up on Michael."

"I've changed my mind. Beth doesn't deserve him."

Jory slowed the car, taking an exit back toward north Tampa. "And you say I'm fickle," she said. "Now that Brad's graduated and Ric's out of the picture, what's Melissa going to do with her libido?"

"Absolutely nothing," Melissa said. "I told you, it's books and studying for me. College scholarships are my only true loves."

Jory shook her head. "Which brings us full circle. Melissa chasing substance . . . Jory chasing rainbows."

Melissa squeezed Jory's arm. "Chase the rainbows for both of us."

The tone of urgency in her voice gripped Jory's heart. She eyed her friend and bit her lower lip as she noted the look of sadness on Melissa's face. "I will, Melissa," she said, swallowing her fear. "I promise, this will be the very best year any two seniors at Lincoln High ever had. We'll leave 'em laughing. Is it a deal?"

Melissa's eyes softened. "It's a deal."

Jory lowered the car window to allow the humid summer heat inside and combat the sudden chill that had swept through her. "Then how about some lunch?"

"It's ten o'clock. We just had breakfast."

"Correction. You and Michael and Beth just had breakfast. I didn't eat a thing."

Melissa laughed, and Jory drove into a fast-food drive-thru lane laughing too. *The best senior year ever.* She'd made Melissa a promise she would keep. No matter what.

Chapter Four

The start of school wasn't nearly as exciting as Jory had hoped. The halls looked the same, the classes were just as boring, the faces of new freshmen just as bewildered and lost-looking. There were no seniors to look up to, either. "We're it," she'd told Melissa after the first day of classes. "So why don't I feel important?"

It was lonely coming home to an empty house, too. Except for Mrs. Garcia, who cooked and dusted and kept the place immaculate, the house seemed lifeless and hollow. Jory almost began to miss her mother's constant nagging. A few postcards describing the "beauty of the Thames" and the "rugged Irish Moors" were all she had to remind her that she did have parents.

Jory went to Melissa's often. First out of loneliness, then, once her parents returned, out of a need to escape, and by mid-September her days had settled into a monotonous routine. She was at Melissa's the afternoon her friend received a letter notifying her that she'd been named a National Merit semifinalist. "Didn't I say you would be one?" Jory asked with an indulgent expression.

Melissa was stunned and continued to look

dazed, even after Jory had poured her a cola and ushered her to the pine table in the Austin's kitchen. "I . . . I should call Mom at work . . ."

"Catch your breath first." Jory took the letter, read it aloud, and hugged Melissa. "How does it feel to have a dream come true?"

"Anticlimactic. What do I do for an encore?"

"Get one of the scholarships. According to the letter, they notify school principals in February who the finalists are and then award the scholarships in March and April." She glanced up from the letter, her green eyes wide with respect. "It says here that only fifteen thousand high school juniors in the *entire* country get to be semifinalists. I'm impressed, Melissa."

Melissa's face broke into an ear-to-ear grin. "So all I have to do now is score incredibly high on the SATs, get a teacher to write a glowing recommendation on my finalist application, and not let any of my grades fall this school year." She snapped her fingers. "A cinch."

And keep going for chemotherapy and hope that your cancer doesn't go out of remission. Jory heard the unwelcome thought inside her head as loudly as if it had been spoken. "When they go public with the names of the kids who made semifinalists and print your name in the *Tampa Tribune*, you'll become a celebrity," she said.

"Fame, but no fortune," Melissa mused. "Four years of college is expensive." She waved the letter under Jory's nose. "This is my only hope."

Jory felt guilty because she knew she could afford to attend any university or college she wanted, grades permitting. "So where will you apply? Yale?"

Melissa arched her eyebrow. "You mean because Brad's there? If you recall, dear-but-meddling-Jory, Brad Kessing had a girlfriend when he left for college. You *do* remember Sarah of the golden hair and innocent blue eyes, don't you?"

Jory wrinkled her nose. "She was so All-American clean, she squeaked."

Melissa laughed. "And even if Brad and Sarah are no longer an item, I'm certain he's discovered some gorgeous Vassar girl by now."

"Then why don't you apply to Vassar?" Jory asked brightly.

"I'm over Brad. And before you go spending all my scholarship money, how about if I first win the scholarship?"

"You will. But you're right—first things first." Jory scrunched her brow. "To celebrate this first coup—becoming a semifinalist—we need to have a party."

"Jory . . ."

"I'll throw the party. It'll be a bash—a blowout!" Jory rubbed her hands together, warming to her plan. "A beach party," she said, slapping her hand against the table with a smack.

"Now, you know I can't be out in the sun."

"There's no sun at night," Jory countered. "Water's still there. Sand is still warm. We can build a bonfire, roast hot dogs, marshmallows, maybe a few senior boys . . ."

"The beach at night? Bonfires? It's illegal."

"Don't be a party pooper. My parents own a strip of beach real estate south of Clearwater that they're selling for condos, so it's private property and we can do whatever we like."

"But it's almost October . . ."

"So what?" Jory interrupted. "This is the *perfect* time of year for a beach party. Not too muggy. Not too cold. I'm telling you, it's perfect." She took a long sip of cola, her brain tumbling with ideas. "And besides, it's my party. And I want to give it in your honor."

Melissa squirmed. "It's too much fuss . . ."

"I don't think so. Anyway, how will I maintain my party girl image this year at school if I don't whoop it up once in a while?"

"But I thought you were going to get serious about your life."

"I've got forever to get serious about the rest of my life. I only have one senior year."

Melissa smiled tentatively. "I guess one party can't hurt . . ."

"Good. Then I'll start making the plans. First, I need to pick a date." Jory stood, crossed to the bulletin board on the kitchen wall, and studied the calendar. "When's your next clinic visit?"

"Two weeks."

Jory wanted plenty of time between the visit and the party. She wanted Melissa feeling her best. She poked the calendar, a Saturday in early November. "This looks like a good date to me. Let's designate it 'P-day.' I'll get the word out."

"Do you suppose anyone will come?"

"Get real, Melissa. Who would refuse an invitation to a party thrown by Jory Delaney?"

"Sorry. It was a momentary lapse into insanity," Melissa giggled.

"Then it's settled. I'll throw a party. And believe me, it will be a party to remember. Lincoln will be talking about this party long after we're dead and gone . . ." The innocent words were out of her mouth before she could stop them. *Dead and gone*. What a stupid thing to say.

Melissa offered a wistful smile. "We all die, Jory. You don't have to feel bad about reminding me. Forget it."

Jory nodded, still fighting the prickly sensations that were turning her face red and making her squirm. "Anyway, it'll be a great party. Trust me."

"Of course it will. What else would I expect from my best friend?"

Jory's mother was less enthusiastic about Jory's party. "The beach at night? On our property? Really, Jory, can't you come up with a better idea? Why not the country club?"

Jory wrinkled her nose in disdain. "These are the 'common folks,' Mom. We want to have fun, not be hemmed in at some snobby club."

"But on our property? It's so isolated. There's nothing out there for miles. What about legal liabilities? And what about chaperons?"

Jory clenched her teeth but forced a sweet

smile. "I'll get everyone to sign waivers for your insurance company."

"Don't be a smart-mouth. You know what I mean."

Mrs. Delaney tapped her heel on the thick pile carpet of Jory's bedroom. She crossed her arms over the front of her vivid pink silk shirtwaist dress. "Perhaps we could make a deal."

Jory sensed disaster but asked, "What sort of deal?"

"Gasparilla's coming up in February."

Jory grew wary. Gasparilla was a holiday unique to the Tampa Bay area. In the 1600s, the pirate José Gaspar sailed into the bay and captured the city. For some reason, in later years, the socially prominent of the city had turned the anniversary of the event into a festival that centered on balls, parties, parades, and even a nationally recognized marathon that garnered some of the world's top runners. The highlight of the day was when a socially elite crew consisting largely of men with Old Tampa money and influence sailed into the bay aboard an authentic pirate ship and "captured the city."

"So what about it?"

"Your father has been invited to be part of the crew this year, and there're umpteen parties and galas for us to attend."

"No reason why you two shouldn't."

"*You're* a part of this family, Jory, and you will be expected to be a part of the festivities."

Every fiber of Jory's being rebelled. "I can't think of anything I'd rather *not* do."

Her mother's face darkened. "This is quite an honor for our family, Jory, and I won't have you spoiling it by your flip attitude toward polite society."

Jory rolled her eyes in indignation. "Well, excuse me."

"Your attitude doesn't make sense, anyway," Mrs. Delaney continued. "You want to give a party, yet you don't want to attend parties for your father's and my sake. Parties where you'll meet the right people, dress in beautiful clothes, and have a wonderful time. Honestly, I just don't understand you."

I know you don't, Mother, Jory thought. "So our taste in parties is different."

"Don't be cute," Mrs. Delaney said shortly. She studied Jory, who lifted her chin defiantly. "Why don't we compromise?" she asked.

"Meaning?"

"I'll let you throw your party on our beach property if you'll cooperate with me over the next few months about the functions I want you to attend."

A warning bell clanged in Jory's head. "I have to keep my grades up," she hedged.

Her mother chuckled derisively. "I'll be certain not to cut into your study time. And the Gasparilla party circuit won't really begin to heat up until after Christmas."

"How many functions?"

"As many as I think appropriate for you."

Jory's temper flared. "That's not fair! I want to give one party and you're locking me into as many as you want."

"Don't act childish, Jory. I'll only accept the invitations I feel will be useful to us and our position in the community."

Her mother's perspective sounded cold and callous and made Jory cringe inwardly. She wondered whom her mother deemed the "right" people for her to mingle with. She knew it wouldn't be the Austins. The thought of her plans to help make this the best year of Melissa's life cooled Jory's anger. "Do you have escorts to these events picked out for me?"

"Of course not. Not until I know which specific events you'll be attending. Then we'll decide. But I won't stick you with losers, Jory. It'll be only the nicest of young men." .

I'll bet, Jory thought bitterly. An image of Michael floated into her mind. *Definitely not the right type*. But what did it matter? Michael was the impossible dream and always had been. But the hopes and plans Jory had for Melissa were not impossible. Her mother was right—all it took was a little compromise. "And once Gasparilla's over, the deal's off?" she asked.

"Please don't make it sound so cut-and-dried. This is for your own good, even if you can't see it now."

My own good . . . Jory was glad that the custom of arranged marriages was no longer in vogue. "All right, Mother. I'll make the trade, but don't bug me about how much time I spend with my other friends." Mrs. Delaney nodded her agreement. "And notify me in plenty of time when one of these little events is coming up. And if I need a special dress for one, you pick it out." Jory knew she was safe in that area. Her mother did have good taste and an infallible sense of style. "And now, please let me have the rest of my senior year to myself."

Mrs. Delaney smoothed the front of her silk dress, and her wrist full of gold bracelets caught the light. Mollified by Jory's compliance, she asked, "How is Melissa, anyway?"

"She's still got cancer." Jory had to clip the words in order not to spit them out. "She gets chemo every six weeks. She gets stuck with needles and has her bone marrow sucked out, and sometimes she gets so sick, she throws up for hours."

A momentary frown knitted Mrs. Delaney's brow. "I am sorry, Jory, that she's having it so rough. I truly am."

"But she does have a shot at a National Merit Scholarship and she's at the top of our class."

"That's nice." Her mother toyed with her jewelry. "I want you to have a good time during your senior year, Jory. I want you to continue your friendship with Melissa. But I also want you to realize how much you have and how much more you can have if you'll only take it."

Her mother had shrugged off Melissa's Merit semifinalist status as if it were nothing. To Jory, the gulf between herself and her mother had never seemed wider. "I'm going to start planning my beach party right away. It'll cost money."

"Money is no problem."

"Right." Jory turned and crossed to her bedroom window, where she lowered the miniblinds against the glare of the sun. To the Delaneys, money never was.

Chapter Five

"Hey, Delaney! Great party."

Jory flashed a smile at the anonymous shout coming from a group of classmates, and shielded her eyes from the glare of sunlight off the bright green water of the gulf. The sun hadn't even set and already the party was in full tilt. She hadn't expected such a huge turnout, but news of the party had spread like wildfire and half the senior class had shown up. The weather had cooperated, still balmy with a dry tropical breeze and only a hint of autumn in the November air.

Jory was making her way through the warm sand toward the food tables when Lyle Vargas fell into step beside her. "How you doing, Jory?"

She glanced up at the thick brown hair that always seemed to be hanging over Lyle's forehead. His eyes were almost amber in the waning light. "Fine."

"Haven't seen much of you since school started."

"Been busy." She recalled telling Melissa that she thought he was boring. Actually, she didn't know him at all, except that he had a reputation for being smart and friendly. He played on the varsity basketball team, although he was never a starter, and he'd been on the Brain Bowl team with Melissa the year before. Jory had actually caught him staring at her a few times in the halls at school or at parties.

"It was good news about Melissa's making the National Merit semis, huh?"

Lyle's comment both surprised and touched her. Jory doubted that anyone there even cared that the party was for Melissa's achievements. "I thought so." They passed through a pickup volleyball game and dodged the ball as it smacked the sand in front of them. She stopped at the food tables long enough to grab a cola out of a washtub of ice. "Have you seen Melissa?" She asked a group of girls.

"I saw her heading down the beach with Tony Perez," someone answered.

Jory strained to see down the shoreline in the fading light. She searched vainly for the familiar sight of her friend, but saw only gentle waves lapping the hard white sand.

"Looking for Melissa?"

With a start, Jory realized that Lyle had spoken. She'd almost forgotten that he'd walked with her. Slightly embarrassed, Jory said, "Melissa's seemed out of it ever since I picked her up this afternoon and brought her to the party."

"Yeah. I noticed that too."

"I can't figure out what's got her down."

"She'll probably be back in a few minutes," Lyle offered in a way that made Jory suspect that he understood Jory's concern about her friend's absence better than the average person.

Before she could comment, Pam Hughes interrupted. "Jory, some of the guys are building the bonfire. Where're the hot dogs?"

"I'll get them." Jory turned to Lyle. "Catch you later. Okay?"

His expression fell, but he agreed and wandered off toward the volleyball match. She rummaged through the ice chests shoved beneath the tables. By the time she'd dragged the Styrofoam box to the hollowed-out pit in the sand, the heaped-up firewood was glowing brightly. Several guys were toasting their accomplishment with beer.

Jory frowned, wishing they'd left the beer behind, but knowing it appeared at every party even though no one was of legal age. *Except Michael.* Where had that thought come from? Michael Austin was miles away, and she'd done everything she could to keep from thinking about him for months. Jory sighed and wondered again where Melissa had disappeared to. When she saw Tony Perez dancing with Felicia Garton, she grew concerned. "Tony, have you seen Melissa?"

"Not since we got here."

"I thought you two went for a walk."

"We did, but she told me to go on back, that she'd rather be by herself for a while."

This doesn't sound right, Jory thought. Melissa had been looking forward to the party and had even helped shop for the food. "Which way did she head?"

The dark-haired boy offered an annoyed shrug. "Lighten up, Jory. She'll be back."

"Which way?"

He pointed southward and Jory headed down the beach in an easy jog. Her bare feet slapped the sand, the gentle wash of salt water occasionally brushing over her toes. The sounds of the party receded in the night, and soon all she saw when she looked behind her was the glow of the bonfire. Jory tugged her windbreaker to her, grateful that she'd taken the time to put it on.

The moon came out, only half full, but bright enough to cast an eerie light on the sand. Scattered seashells caught the moonlight and glittered, moist and cool. Jory felt her pulse quicken and her tension evaporate when she saw Melissa sitting alone in the sand, her knees pulled up to her chest, her chin resting on them. Her waist-length hair fluttered in the breeze.

Slowing, pausing for breath, Jory approached her friend. "Is this seat taken?"

Melissa turned slowly and gazed upward. If she was surprised to see Jory, she didn't show it. "No. Sit next to me."

Jory obliged, plopping down with a long exhalation and crossing her legs. Questions crowded her mind. She resisted the urge to be irritated with Melissa for going off without a word. Instead she stared out at the swells and whitecaps, and the lull of the surf calmed her.

Melissa asked, "Why does the ocean always make you feel small and insignificant?"

"Maybe because we are," Jory answered with a shrug. She wasn't in the mood to delve into the mysteries of the universe. "You're missing a good party," she ventured cautiously.

"I'll head back in a few minutes."

They fell silent. Jory sensed that something was wrong, but couldn't bring herself to ask what just yet. "Tony Perez is cute. You took a walk with him?"

"A short walk." There was silence. "Do you ever wonder where God is, Jory?"

"He's in heaven," Jory said matter-of-factly. "What does it matter?"

"I've been thinking about Him lately. I wonder what part He plays in our lives. Do you think He knows us by name? And if He does know each of our names—does that give Him the right to pull us around like we're puppets on strings?"

"I hadn't ever thought about it. It seems to me that He'd be too busy with things like world hunger and world peace and stuff like that to have time for plain old me." Jory picked up a shell and scooped out a hollow in the sand. Loose grains immediately filled the hole and she abandoned the project as hopeless. "Let's see. . . . Does God have a long list with everybody's name on it and check us off one by one?" Jory attempted to lighten Melissa's mood.

"You've got God mixed up with Santa Claus, Jory. No, I think God plans what's going to happen to us even before we're born."

Jory wrinkled her nose in dissatisfaction. "Doesn't sound like we get much of a chance to make decisions about our lives, huh?"

"No. Therefore, I guess it doesn't really matter if we're good or bad, does it? God's already decided what's going to happen to us."

"Now *you're* making Him sound like Santa Claus." Jory poked Melissa's arm playfully. "I don't know why you're thinking such heavy thoughts, but personally, I think everybody gets a choice about how he wants to manage his own life. You either do what's right or you do what's wrong. But I'll bet God knows what choice you're gonna make before you do. That makes sense to me. How about you?"

"But what about the things that just happen to people. Things you don't get a choice about? Does God decide those things for you in advance?"

Like getting cancer, Jory thought, the conversation weighing her down. A fiddler crab ventured out of his burrow and scampered to the waterline. A wave broke offshore, sending a rush of water toward him. He attempted a retreat, but the water caught him, tumbled him wildly, and pulled him out to the sea. "So what did God decide about us?" Jory asked lightly, wanting to chase away the unanswerable and the unfathomable. "You're the National Merit scholar."

Melissa turned her face toward Jory. Her eyes were dark hollows and her skin looked pale, ethereal. "God decided that you're going to be rich and famous."

"No kidding? And I just thought I had to figure

out what to do over the rest of the school year." She smiled nervously and pushed her hair behind her ear. "What did He decide for you?"

A wry smile hovered on Melissa's lips. She leaned sideways and whispered from the corner of her mouth, "That I'll go to my grave a virgin."

Jory laughed at Melissa's sudden turn to humor. "Not if Tony Perez has anything to say about it, you won't."

Melissa sobered and pulled the luxurious length of hair over her shoulder and stroked it. "Last spring, when Ric asked me to go to bed with him, it was the funniest feeling. I mean, I wanted to. I really did. I wanted to know what it felt like. To be with a guy that way." Jory squirmed in the sand. She'd seen enough movies and read enough books to have wondered the same thing. "But in the end, I decided I wanted more than to just satisfy my curiosity. I wanted to be in love."

Bewildered, Jory still couldn't figure out where the conversation was leading. "I guess we all want to be in love before we try making love. I know I do." Sometimes she thought she was in love with Michael, but he'd never even so much as held her. "So maybe when you get to college, you'll fall in love. I have to agree that it's slim pickings in our senior class."

Melissa leaned back on her palms and let her head drop back. In the moonlight Jory could see she looked troubled, and she realized that Melissa still hadn't touched on what was really bothering her. "So we've talked about God and love. What else? We need to get back to the party before they send out a search party."

"Do you think they've even missed us? Do you think anyone even cares?"

"Of course," Jory volunteered. "In fact, Lyle Vargas was asking about you. He seems more sensitive than most of the clods in our crowd."

Melissa smiled. "If he asked about me, it was just an excuse to have a conversation with you."

Jory waved her hand. "Sure. All the guys like Jory but the right one."

"You're a good friend, Jory, and the party's super."

"How would you know? You've missed practically the whole thing."

"I got a call from the clinic today."

Jory started. Her breath caught in her throat, and her heart began to hammer. *A call from the clinic.* "And?"

"And they said that my blood work showed signs of an elevated white count again."

Jory licked her lips nervously but her mouth was dry. "An infection?"

Melissa faced her, and immediately she was hidden in shadows. "It means I'm out of remission. It means my leukemia has come back."

Chapter Six

"There must be some mistake," Jory said. "They must have gotten your lab work mixed up with someone else's. Why, I saw a story on TV just the other day about a woman whose baby got mixed up with another woman's in a hospital nursery. I mean, if they can get a real live baby mixed up, what chance do they have with a blood sample?" Jory knew she was babbling, but she couldn't stop.

"There's no mistake, Jory."

"Well then, they've just misinterpreted the results. Maybe you really do have an infection. Infections can cause white blood counts to go up. I know for a fact . . ."

Melissa laid her hand on Jory's arm. "It's not an infection. It's a relapse."

Jory struggled to her feet, agitated, restless. Her legs had cramped from sitting so long and she stumbled when she tried to pace. "Well, I don't believe it. You've been feeling great for ages. You look terrific too. They've made a mistake." She was angry at the nameless, faceless doctors who were ruining Melissa's life.

Melissa stood and dusted off the seat of her

jeans. "It's all right, Jory. You don't have to be so upset about it."

Jory whirled. "No it isn't all right. Now you've got to start that stinking chemo stuff again. You'll lose your hair. You'll be sick all the time."

"No chemo this time, Jory."

Jory halted her tirade and stared at Melissa's face. She realized that she was seeing Melissa through a mist of tears. "The chemo worked the first time. Why won't they do it again?"

"Because achieving second remissions with chemo is difficult."

"Then what will they do?"

"Dr. Rowan says they want to try a bone marrow transplant."

Jory had heard the term when Melissa had first been diagnosed a year before, but she couldn't remember what the treatment involved. "Tell me about it."

"It's when they take healthy bone marrow from a donor and put it into my cancerous bone marrow. The theory is that the new marrow will begin to grow and take over from the bad marrow, and I'll be cured."

"Why didn't they do that to begin with?"

Jory watched Melissa shove a seashell around with her big toe. "It's risky."

"How risky?"

"Fifty-fifty chance of its working."

The implications of Melissa's words momentarily tied Jory's tongue. Finally she said, "Sounds like they're calling a coin toss. Heads, they win. Tails, you lose."

"That's about the size of it."

"And if they don't do the transplant at all? What are the odds then of your being cured?"

"Twenty percent."

"Stinking odds." She took a long, shuddering breath and faced Melissa fully, crossing her arms as if to ward off the impracticality of the math equation. "So where do you get this marrow?"

"Dr. Rowan says that anyone's best chance comes when the marrow is received from a biologically compatible donor."

"Meaning?"

"Michael."

Jory's heart lurched. *Double jeopardy.* What if they both lost? "Is it dangerous?"

"More for Michael than for me. For him, it means an operation to remove the marrow and a recovery period. There's a risk whenever anyone goes under general anesthesia. It's uncomfortable for the donor because they put a needle into his hipbone to extract the marrow."

Jory trembled and for a second felt queasy. "Then what happens?"

"Once they remove it, they bring the marrow to me in IV bags and let it drip into me, just like the chemo. I'm awake the whole time and won't feel anything. Mom can even sit with me. We can read

or play Monopoly. 'Do not pass Go. Do not collect
$200' . . ." Her attempt at humor didn't help Jory.

"How does Michael feel about donating his
marrow?"

"You know Michael. . . . Bring on the lions."

Jory smiled wistfully, thinking of Michael. "You
said there were risks," she said.

"Well, it's more complicated than just dumping
Michael's marrow into my body. It has to do with
genetic compatibility."

"I thought you said you and Michael were compatible."

"We are. Mostly. But there's always the threat
of rejection. And complications."

"You could reject his marrow?"

"Our cells' genetic codes are different. My
body will attack his marrow the minute it gets inside."

"But I'll bet the doctors have a solution for that
problem too." Jory knew she sounded sarcastic, but
she didn't care.

"How'd you guess?" Melissa stooped and
picked up the shell and ran her fingers over the
smooth, sea-worn surface. "They put me in the hospital and do testing to see if I'm a candidate for the
operation in the first place. If so, they put me into
isolation, in a germ-free room, and start me on massive doses of autoimmune suppressant drugs. They
destroy my body's ability to fight germs, *and* it's
ability to fight off Michael's bone marrow. Then
they do the transplant. Then we have to wait to see
if it takes, and hope there aren't any complications,

like a secondary infection. As I understand it, even a common cold could kill me because I'll have no resistance to fight it."

"And if it does take?"

"I get to go home and go on a different kind of maintenance program. Ultimately, I can be cured."

She cleared her throat. "So how long will all this testing and suppressing and operating take?"

"Six to eight weeks."

"So if you go in now, you could be out by January."

"I haven't said I'd do it."

"What?" Jory leaned forward, as if she hadn't heard correctly. "I don't understand."

Melissa flung the shell far into the sea. It shattered the path the moonlight made on the water. "It's my body and my treatment, and I haven't decided to go ahead with it."

"But . . . you have to!" Jory's eyes grew wide, her palms clammy. "The odds . . ."

"Screw the odds." Melissa's voice had gone calm and steely. "I'm not sure I want to be part of some grand experiment."

"But they must do this operation all the time. I read where they transplant whole hearts and livers. Surely a little bone marrow—"

Melissa interrupted. "But this time it's *me*, Jory. It's not some stranger in the newspaper."

"What are you gonna do?" Jory couldn't keep her voice from wavering as she asked the question.

"I don't know . . . Which brings us back to our original discussion, doesn't it? Maybe God's already decided what I'm going to do. Just like He decided that I was going to have leukemia."

Jory felt the darkness of the night closing in on her. She was afraid. Afraid because she could do no more to change the course of Melissa's life than she could to change the course of the tide. "You will tell me when you decide, won't you? No matter what you decide?"

Melissa hooked her arm through Jory's. "You know I will. You're my best friend."

Jory felt a lump wedged in her throat. "Come back to the party with me and I'll roast you a marshmallow."

"You're on."

They walked together slowly toward the party and the bonfire's flaming fingers. As they walked the water washed their footprints away leaving no trace of their existence on the shell-strewn beach.

"Your father's furious, Jory. How do you think we felt when the police showed up at two A.M. to tell us that they'd busted a bunch of minors for drinking on our beach property?"

Jory faced her mother in the luxurious living room of their house, too weary to do much more than shift from foot to foot. "For the tenth time, Mother, I left at midnight to take Melissa home and I didn't go back to the party. I just came on home."

"But it was *your* responsibility and *your* friends."

"I said I was sorry."

"Sorry doesn't cut it. We allowed you to throw that party, but we'd never condone drinking by minors."

Jory knew she should have hung around and supervised the party, but after hearing Melissa's latest news, neither of them had been in the mood for it. "Look, I'll go back today and make sure the property is cleaned up. I never meant for things to get out of hand."

"It's going to be a long time before we allow you to have another party, Jory, so don't ask." Mrs. Delaney glared and tapped her nails on the marble mantle of the fireplace.

Jory sighed, impatient to escape her mother's foul temper. She didn't know what else to say. She couldn't tell her about Melissa's problems because her friend had asked Jory to keep it secret until she decided what she wanted to do about the transplant. "Don't worry. It'll be a long time before I want to throw another party. Can I go now?"

"Not yet. I want to discuss your schedule for the upcoming holiday season."

"What schedule?"

"The party agenda and where we'll be expected to attend."

Jory groaned. "Do I have to?"

"Yes, you do. There's a dinner dance at the University Club that highly placed educators from all over the state will be attending. I told Beverly Hotchkiss that her son Steve could escort you."

Jory rolled her eyes, remembering Steve as

conceited and mouthy with roaming hands. "Not him," she groaned.

"Beverly's husband chairs the state committee on education and is very influential. For a girl who may need all the influence she can gather simply to get into college, this particular party is a must."

"Kids get into college on their grades and test scores, Mother, not on who they know."

"Don't you bet on it," Mrs. Delaney said. "Besides I think your father has his sights set on your attending the University of Miami, his alma mater."

Jory's mouth dropped open. Her parents had already decided her future! "Since when? Cripes, I haven't even made up my mind about *going* to college yet. That's not fair!"

"We're only trying to do what's best for you, Jory. If you do decide to go to college, at least this way you'll have your foot in the door. Your father's already begun your paperwork."

"How dare you and Daddy do this without my permission!"

"Why can't you see that we are not your enemies, Jory? We only want what's best for you."

Jory felt that the world was crumbling. Melissa was facing a risky cure, Jory was expected to date boys she disliked and go to parties she didn't want to attend, and her parents were negotiating her life like a real estate deal. "You can't *make* me do something I don't want to do," she said stubbornly. "And I still haven't made up my mind about college, much less where I want to go. So stop it!"

"Well make it up," Mrs. Delaney said, her tone angry. "Decide something by January, because that's all the time I'm going to give you to start being sensible about the rest of your life."

Chapter Seven

On Monday, the school was buzzing about Jory's party and the raid by the police. Without meaning to, she'd achieved minor celebrity status at Lincoln. "What did they do to you?" she asked a group of guys at lunch.

Billy Warren lowered his dark glasses and grinned. "Not half of what my dad did to me. I'm on probation until 1999."

"Glad you can make light of it, Warren," another boy said. "I got my car taken away and I'm walking to school for the rest of the semester."

Jory propped her elbows on the table and rested her chin on her palms. "Sorry it got out of hand."

Billy shrugged. "It was still a cool party, Jory, so don't sweat it. The cops have us going before a judge next month and we'll probably all be assigned some sort of community service."

"I guess it could be worse," she told him. "Maybe it won't go on your record." After the guys left, she found herself sitting alone with Lyle Vargas. "You get busted too?"

"No. I left before the action started."

"Smart move."

"Why'd you and Melissa leave so early?"

She was surprised that he'd noticed when she'd taken off. "Melissa was tired and she wanted to leave." It was a half-truth, but the whole truth wasn't any of his business.

"Are you her keeper?"

Jory sat up and stared him straight in the eyes. "What's that crack supposed to mean? No, I'm not her keeper, but she's my friend and she's sick and I brought her to the party. When she wanted to go, I took her home. That's all."

Lyle's expression was serious. "When we were on the Brain Bowl team together, I saw how much determination she had and I admired it. I feel sorry for her too."

"I don't feel sorry for her." Jory bristled. "I respect her. She knows what she wants and she goes after it. *She's* a National Merit semifinalist," she added pointedly.

Lyle grinned sheepishly. "So am I."

He caught Jory completely off guard and she felt herself blush. "Congratulations," she said. Then a thought occurred to her. Lyle was brilliant. Would he be capable of taking away a scholarship from Melissa? "Are you applying for a scholarship?" she asked.

"Yeah. I'd like to go to medical school. How about you?"

Jory suddenly felt nervous. She'd never considered that someone else from Lincoln might get the award. She decided not to say anything to Melissa, since her friend had so much else on her mind, but she *would* keep tabs on Lyle. He wasn't bad-looking, Jory thought. A bit serious, but tall and lean with an angular face and intense amber eyes. He was no Michael, but he was handsome in his own way. "I haven't decided where I'll go," she said. "Maybe the University of Miami."

"It's a good school."

"It's close to the beach."

"I haven't decided where I'll go either. A lot depends on getting a scholarship. Even if I don't get the National Merit, I need to get some sort of scholarship, and since I want to be a doctor, I need to do pretty well wherever I end up going."

She shrugged, feeling irritated. Did everybody in the world know what he wanted from life except her? "It takes years and years to become a doctor," she said. "I couldn't stand all that studying. That's the problem with college—you have to study. Maybe I'll just go for the frat parties."

"You can have anything you go after," Lyle said, his eyes holding hers.

"Thanks for the vote of confidence. I'll keep it in mind." She shifted, feeling self-conscious. "I've got to scoot. If I cut one more English class, I'll flunk this six-week grading period."

Lyle scrambled up when she stood. "Maybe we can talk again, Jory."

"Sure, Lyle. Sometime." Jory hurried off to class without a backward glance.

Jory had a fling with Doug Swanson during football playoffs, which kept the next few weekends tied up, but by Thanksgiving, the infatuation had run its course. On Thanksgiving Day, she ate a quick and boring meal with her parents at a restaurant, then went to Melissa's to watch the college games.

Sunk in a comfy beanbag chair, Jory was profoundly aware of Michael stretched out on the sofa near her. He seemed to have returned to his solitary ways and Jory was secretly glad that his relationship with Beth had broken off.

"Popcorn?" Melissa asked, passing Jory an oversized bowl of buttered white kernels.

"I can't eat one more thing."

"Not even chocolate chip cookies? Mom's got a batch in the oven."

"On Thanksgiving Day?"

"She bakes when she's agitated," Melissa said, but offered no other explanation.

"Chocolate chip cookies? Well . . . maybe I could force one down."

Melissa rose from a matching beanbag. "I thought so. I'll be back in a flash."

Alone in the room with Michael, Jory attempted to concentrate on the game, but it was a losing battle.

"What do you think she'll do?" Michael's abrupt question startled her.

"Do about what?" Jory sat up and faced him.

"About the bone marrow transplant. I know she's told you about it."

Jory nodded. "But she hasn't made up her mind yet."

"You'd tell me if she had, wouldn't you? I know she tells you everything."

"Yes, I would," Jory said.

"I mean, it involves me too. It's my bone marrow."

"I think it's a great thing you'd be doing."

"I'd give her my right arm if I thought it would make her well."

Jory heard his anguish and longed to comfort him. If only she had the nerve to put her arms around him. "I know what you mean," she said.

Michael snapped, "How could you? She's just your friend. She's *my* sister. Why are you so helpful to Melissa, anyway? What's in it for Jory?"

His sudden animosity surprised and stung her. "Nothing's in it for me, Michael. I . . . I just care. That's all."

Michael stood abruptly and paced. "Some people get positive strokes from helping life's underdogs," he said accusingly.

Jory's temper flared. "Is that what you think? That I get some sort of kick out of hanging around Melissa?"

"Look at yourself, Jory. You've got money and a rich family and you can have most anything you want. Why Melissa?"

She wanted to shout, "Because she's like a sister to me. Because your family has been more of a family to me than my own. Because I love you, Michael!" Instead, she said, "Sometimes there's no explaining why you like some people more than others. It's just the way things are."

Michael raked his fingers through his black, disheveled hair and rocked back on his heels. "Forget it, Jory. I didn't mean to take it out on you. It's just that I can't stand this waiting around."

"Melissa needs time to decide, Michael. It's not something she can change her mind about half-way through."

"I know, dammit. It's all or nothing." He rotated his shoulders and pressed his eyes closed. "If she tells you first," he asked hesitantly, "if she says anything to you, let me know. Please."

Jory almost reached out and touched him, but instead tucked her hand into the pocket of her jeans. "Okay. But I don't think she will. I think she'll tell you first. You're her brother."

"I'm going for a drive," Michael said. "Tell Melissa to let Mom know. Tell them not to wait up. I'll be gone for a long time."

Jory watched him leave and felt like crying.

Jory and Melissa went Christmas shopping the next day. "Biggest sale day of the year," Jory said as they plowed through the crowded department store in the mall. "Did you bring your list?"

"Yes, but I can't stop long enough to fish it out or I'll get trampled."

"Where's your sense of adventure? Come on. There's a sale rack of sweaters and jeans."

An hour later, Jory led Melissa to the food area in the center of the mall for a soda. She heaped their packages on a chair and sat next to Melissa.

"What a ratrace. Have we gotten through your list yet?"

"I've got a blouse for Mom and two tapes for Michael." Melissa paused. "Remember last year? I was in the hospital and you had to do my shopping for me."

Jory remembered. Melissa had been receiving chemo and she'd lost her hair and was sick as a dog. Jory had brought everything back to the hospital for Melissa's approval. "I did a good job, didn't I?" Jory asked, above the babble of voices around them.

"Michael still wears that cologne you picked out."

The mention of Michael made Jory recall his hostility toward her and she gave an offhanded shrug. "I had fun choosing it."

"Wonder what we'll be doing this time next year."

"Shopping, of course."

"Will we?" Melissa withdrew her straw from the cola and let a few drops puddle on the table.

A shiver went up Jory's spine. Melissa's mood swings were frustrating. One minute she was involved and happy, the next minute she was distracted and pensive. "We've done this post-Thanksgiving ritual for four years," Jory reminded her.

"Except last year."

"Ah, come on, Scrooge, where's your Christmas spirit? We'll be here shopping again next year. We were born to shop!"

"I might not get home for Thanksgiving, depending on where I go to school."

"That's a possibility," Jory said.

"Then again, if I don't get a scholarship . . ."

They stopped talking because Jory wasn't convinced they were really discussing Christmas shopping. From speakers, Christmas music played. A small ficus tree stood decorated with white lights and the stores were decorated with bright green plastic wreaths with red bows. Suddenly the mall looked too bright. There were too many people and too much noise. "You want to get out of here?" Jory asked.

Melissa plucked at her straw with her thumbnail. "Would you take me someplace special if I asked you?"

"You know I will. Name it."

"Don't freak out on me, all right?"

Puzzled, Jory began to gather up her packages. "Would you like to drive over to the beach? It's chilly, but at least the sun's shining."

"Not the beach." Melissa caught Jory's eyes and held them. "I want you to take me to Memorial Gardens. I want to visit Rachael Dove's grave."

Chapter Eight

～～

The grounds of the cemetery were beautifully kept, and a gravel road wound through sections of headstones and monuments. A cloudless blue sky stretched overhead and the afternoon sun warded off a chill in the air. "Are you sure you want to do this?" Jory asked, driving slowly in the direction of Rachael's gravesite.

Melissa glanced up from the map she'd been given at the entrance. "I'm sure. Take a left."

Jory obeyed, but didn't like the idea one bit. She'd never met the four-year-old Rachael and knew of her only through Melissa. Yet she did remember how devastated Melissa had been when the child had died the previous spring. Rachael had given Melissa a page from her Cinderella coloring book and it was still pinned to her bedroom bulletin board. "This place is creepy, Melissa."

"I don't think so. I think it's sort of restful."

"*Too* restful for me."

"Stop, Jory," Melissa directed. "I think it's over there, by that tree."

Melissa was out of the car before Jory could turn off the engine. By the time she caught up, her friend had found the bronze marker with Rachael's name on it. Jory eyed the embossed rose at the bottom. It seemed indecent to see the dates of Rachael's birth and death—too short a time span lay between the two numbers. Other markers stretched row upon row, in both directions. The plots seemed small and crowded together. "You ready to go yet?" Jory licked her lips nervously.

"Not yet." Melissa stared down for several minutes before she spoke. "I read a poem in English Lit. last month by Gerard Manley Hopkins called 'Spring and Fall.'"

"Could we discuss this someplace else?"

Melissa continued as if she hadn't heard Jory speak. "It was about a little girl named Margaret who's crying becuase the leaves die in autumn. I don't remember it word for word. But the last part goes, 'Now no matter, child, the name: Sorrow's springs are the same. . . . It is the blight man was born for, It is Margaret you mourn for.'"

Jory felt goose bumps on her arms. "We're all born to die. Is that it?"

"So it seems," Melissa said.

"Are you going to have the transplant?" Jory asked quietly.

Melissa's eyes were wide and troubled. "I don't know. I'm scared, Jory. Real scared."

"I'm scared too."

"My doctor said he found lymphoblasts in my blood work last time. The chemo isn't doing the trick for me anymore."

"The transplant *is* a chance," Jory observed.

"They shut me in a sterile room, Jory, with machines and monitors."

"Can you have visitors?"

"Yes, but everyone who comes in has to dress in those sterile green hospital gowns and wear a mask."

"I look good in green," Jory ventured, hoping to break the tension.

Melissa looked around the cemetery. "This might be the only way out of that room for me, Jory."

Jory swallowed hard. "Maybe not. Maybe you'll beat the odds."

"Rachael didn't."

"But you're not Rachael. And she didn't have a bone marrow transplant."

Melissa nodded slowly. "That's true."

"You can lick this thing, Melissa," Jory said. "I know you can. Didn't I predict you'd be a National Merit semifinalist? Didn't you beat the odds on that?"

"Yes."

"Then you can do it again."

Melissa sighed and gazed up at the bright blue sky. "We can go now," she said.

When Jory got home she called Doug, even though they weren't dating anymore. "There's a party over on Davis Island," she told him, forcing a happy voice. "Want to go?" They ended up at a mansion with white pillars and a circular, shrub-lined driveway.

"Who owns this place?" Doug asked in genuine awe.

"Friend of a friend." Jory led him inside, where music screamed and kids danced in tight bunches, shouting above the noise. She wanted to laugh and dance and have a ball. She wanted to forget about the cemetery and Rachael and Margaret, the girl in the poem. Doug nuzzled her neck, but she shied away. "Cool it, Doug."

"Well, excuse me. I thought we were here to have a good time." He tried again to pull her close.

"I plan to have a good time, but hands off. Okay?"

"What's with you, Jory? First you're hot, then you're cold. I don't like being jerked around."

Jory stepped out of Doug's grasp. "Look, this was a bad idea. I don't really feel like partying after all, but there's no reason you shouldn't stay." Before he could do anything, Jory escaped into the crowd and headed for the door.

Once outside she took in big gulps of air and squeezed her eyes shut, because she suddenly felt like crying. "You're being stupid," she told herself aloud. "You like parties. Parties like you." But no matter what she said, she felt only like going home and being by herself.

The atmosphere at the Austin's dinner table was tense. For Jory, it didn't seem much like Christmas Eve. Melissa was withdrawn, Michael was sullen and brooding, and Mrs. Austin was overly chatty, insisting everyone have seconds, when they hadn't even finished their firsts.

"Tell me, Jory, what's your family planning for Christmas Day?"

"My mother's got a party lined up in the late afternoon. I'm not sure where." She did, but hated thinking about spending a tedious afternoon with her parents' friends. Naturally, Mrs. Delaney had seen to it that a "charming young man" would be there for Jory. Their fight over it still rang in her ears, but she was going.

"I was thinking that we might go to a movie," Mrs. Austin said. "You know how long Christmas Day can be. After the gifts are unwrapped and the dinner's eaten, what's left to do?"

Jory envied Mrs. Austin's plans. There were no parties to attend, just family togetherness. She'd have given a million dollars to go to that movie with them.

"Would you like more lasagna, Michael?"

"No, thanks. I'm full."

"But you hardly ate anything and it's your favorite—"

"No, Mom." His abruptness caused a strained silence to fall.

"This isn't fair." Melissa spoke. "Everybody's on edge and it's all my fault."

"That's not so . . ." Mrs. Austin began.

Melissa slammed her fork against her plate. "Yes it is. This is Christmas Eve and it's worse than a funeral around here." She backed away from the table and left the kitchen. Michael exchanged glances with his mother and the two of them hurried after her. Jory had no choice but to follow.

In the living room, Melissa stood fingering the needles on the decorated Christmas tree. Jory hung back, fidgeting, while Mrs. Austin went to her daughter. "What can I do to help, Melissa? Tell me, please."

"Nothing. There's nothing anybody can do." Melissa's voice was soft and Jory had to inch closer in order to hear.

Michael came up on the other side of his sister. "Remember the Christmas we went to Disney World?"

Melissa nodded. "I was ten and you rode Space Mountain with me and didn't even hassle me afterward when I threw up."

"You never did have a strong stomach."

Melissa turned her head and smiled wistfully at him. "You told me that I should go ride it with you one more time. That it was like falling off a horse. You had to get right back on and ride again." With sudden swiftness, Melissa spun and said to her mother, "What should I do, Mom? Please tell me what to do."

Mrs. Austin held her daughter and stroked her hair, which by now was almost past her jawline. "You're my baby, Melissa. It's killing me watching you have to make this decision. But I believe it's your decision to make. I want you to grow old, Melissa. I can't stand the thought of your not living a full life."

Melissa buried her face in her mother's shoul-

der. "Old and wrinkled sounds wonderful to me."
She pulled away. "But we all know there are no
guarantees if I have the transplant."

Michael cleared his throat and shoved his
hands in his pockets. "Are you saying my bone marrow might not come through? I only manufacture
primo stuff, you know."

"Does it come with a money-back warranty?"
Melissa asked.

"A 'life-back' warranty," he said, his voice
barely above a whisper.

Jory inched toward the door. She felt intrusive,
like an eavesdropper. How differently Mrs. Austin
treated Melissa from the way her mother treated
her. Jory wasn't even allowed to make a simple decision about college, and Melissa was being entrusted
to make one about her very life.

"What do you think, Jory?"

Melissa's question so surprised her, that Jory
felt her cheeks flush, and her feet seemed rooted to
the carpet. Her gaze flitted from face to face. "I . . .
I . . . don't know . . ."

"You once told me that we all get choices about
how we want to manage our lives," Melissa said.

Jory recalled their conversation on the beach.
"I still think that's true." She chose her words carefully because Michael and Mrs. Austin were watching, and her heart was pounding and her palms
were sweating. "It's sort of like if we don't choose
whenever we get the chance, then we have nothing
to complain about if things don't work out the way
we want them to in our hearts."

Melissa shrugged and dropped her eyes, miserably. "I don't feel like I have much of a choice."

Mrs. Austin put her arm around Melissa's shoulders. "I'll support any choice you make."

Jory studied the faces of the three Austins. Same dark hair, blue eyes, and pointed chin. The Christmas tree lights twinkled behind them, making patterns on their skin. She ached inside, longing to be a part of them.

"I'll do it," Melissa said softly. "I'll call Dr. Rowan right after New Year's and tell him I'll do the transplant."

Mrs. Austin sagged with relief and Michael broke out in a grin. "That's a girl," he said. "We'll beat this thing, Melissa. With my marrow and your guts, we're going to win."

Jory walked toward the door, pausing long enough to take one last look at the three of them. Though her heart begged to stay with Melissa and Michael and their mother, her common sense told her she was intruding.

Outside stars burned in the sky, and Christmas lights shone from neighborhood houses. She shivered. In one week her best friend would begin a journey into the unknown. Jory swore to God that, one way or another, she would not go alone.

Chapter Nine

~~~

"Jory, wait up. I want to talk to you."

Jory turned in the school's crowded hallway and spotted Lyle. "What do you want?" She wasn't in a good mood and knew it.

"I heard Melissa is back in the hospital. Is that true?"

"Doesn't anyone have anything else to gossip about around this place?"

"It's not gossip, Jory. I'm interested."

The sincere expression on his face made her regret her sharp remark. "Everybody's asking, Lyle. I'll bet I've been asked about Melissa a million times today." Jory stopped beside a bank of lockers. "She went back right after New Year's. They've been putting her through a bunch of tests and plan to do a bone marrow transplant real soon."

"Are they using her brother's marrow?"

"Yes. But first she has to undergo autoimmune suppression. It'll take a couple of weeks before her body's ready for the marrow. Rejection," Jory said. "That's the problem."

"I'm sorry, Jory. I know she's your friend."

Jory felt tears well in her eyes and she shifted uneasily. "I've got to go."

Lyle's hand shot out and touched her shoulder. "Would you like to go someplace after school and talk about it?"

She shrugged nonchalantly. "What's to talk about? There's nothing to do but wait and hope that the transplant takes."

"You act like it doesn't bother you."

"It bothers me plenty, but I don't go around discussing it with every Tom, Dick, and Harry."

"Or Lyle," he said with a quick smile.

For some reason, his concern made her want to bolt. "The bell's about to ring. Can't be late," she said with forced enthusiasm.

"I wouldn't want to make you late," Lyle said, shifting forward.

She stepped back, feeling a tightness in her chest, and all she wanted to do was get away.

"If you change your mind . . ." Lyle said.

"I won't, but thanks for the offer. I'll be just fine." She forced a carefree smile. "There's plenty to do without sitting around and speculating about Melissa. I'll tell her that you were asking about her, though." Jory stepped into the flow of students, scurrying to class before the morning bell sounded. She smiled and waved to everybody all the way to her classroom.

"Welcome to my clean, germ-free universe. They scrubbed it down with disinfectants and sprayed it with ultraviolet light. What do you think?"

Jory entered Melissa's room through a cubicle,

pushing up the sleeves of an oversized sterile gown. She felt freakish in mask and bonnet. "To quote Kermit the Frog, 'It isn't easy being green,'" she said.

Melissa giggled. "You can always make me laugh, Jory." She was sitting up in bed, but at least she looked normal, not bloated and splotchy as she had the first time she'd been in the hospital undergoing chemo.

Machines and apparatus lined the walls. "Have they started the drugs?" Jory asked, adjusting her mask, thinking her voice sounded muffled.

"Tomorrow." Wires attached to Melissa's chest led to a monitor that registered a regular green blip on a small screen.

"What's that?"

"My heart monitor. There's been some damage to my heart from the chemo. They have to keep close tabs on it."

"And that?" She pointed to a small cart with paddles.

"A crash cart. In case my heart goes haywire." Jory grimaced. Melissa seemed resigned now and, in some ways, eager to get on with the program. She added, "You just missed Michael."

Jory wasn't too sorry she'd missed him. Ever since the day he'd questioned her motives for being involved with his sister, she'd felt awkward around him. Still, it hadn't lessened how deeply she cared for him. "Is he nervous about going under the knife?"

"Worse than a two-year-old. Why are men such babies about needles and hospitals?"

"I wouldn't like it much myself," Jory confessed. "When does he check in?"

"Day before surgery. They prep him early the next morning, extract the marrow, and rush it over here to me. He'll go into the recovery room and then back to his hospital room. They say he'll be up and around in no time. Two or three days, max."

"They probably need the bed for sick people," Jory said with a nervous laugh, because her stomach felt funny whenever she thought about them sticking syringes into Michael's bones.

"I got my SAT scores," Melissa said, changing the subject. "And Mrs. Watson is writing my recommendation for the Merit Scholarship."

The information brought a sense of normalcy into Jory's thoughts. "Mother's making me apply to the University of Miami," she told Melissa.

"Is that what you want?"

"No, but I don't know what I want, so I'm just biding my time and trying to go along with her. Mother can be very determined." She didn't want to burden Melissa with how much the two of them yelled at one another. Jory went on quickly. "A lot of the kids at school are asking about you. Lyle too."

"He likes you, Jory."

Jory looked skeptical. "I don't like him. I mean, not in that way."

"Is it still my brother?"

Jory dropped her gaze and picked at the front of her gown with gloved fingers. "He's angry with me, Melissa. I don't know why either."

"He's angry at everybody. He's been going to a gym and taking it out on a punching bag."

"Doesn't he ever go up in his balloon anymore?"

Melissa shook her head. "No. I wish he would, but it's like he's doing penance. He won't let himself have a good time while I'm sick."

Jory wrinkled her nose. "That's weird. How's that going to help you?"

"Go figure." They fell silent and Jory heard the hiss of some machine and the steady electronic beep of Melissa's heart monitor. Melissa reached into the drawer of her bedside table and withdrew a small book. "Will you do me a favor, Jory?"

"Anything."

"This is my journal." She handed over a blue leather-bound volume. "I've been writing in it ever since last year. I want to keep writing in it. You know, keep a record of these days."

Jory nodded. "Sounds like a good idea. What can I do?"

"If things don't go well . . . if I get real sick or something, keep it up for me."

The request seemed overwhelming and Jory handed the book back to Melissa. "Cripes, I'm no good at that sort of thing. I can't even keep my class notes in order. Maybe your mother could do it for you."

"No. I want you to do it."

"But what would I write?"

"The facts. Your feelings. Whatever you think of."

"Melissa, I can't."

Melissa jutted her lower jaw. "It's important to me, Jory."

"But why?"

Melissa hugged the book to her. "Maybe because it's the only thing I have to leave behind. Rachael Dove left a whole pile of coloring book pages and I know they must mean everything to her family."

"You sound like you don't think this transplant is going to work." The notion irritated Jory. "You've got to think positive, Melissa."

"I believe in the transplant. But I still want you to do this for me."

"But *you'll* do it for now?" Jory licked her lips and felt sweat trickle down between her shoulder blades. The mask was making it difficult to breathe.

"As long as I can."

"And after you're home, you'll keep writing in it?"

Melissa stared at Jory for a long moment. "Sure. Once I'm home."

Jory felt relieved. Once Melissa went home, everything would return to normal. "It's a deal," she said. Melissa slid the book back inside the drawer and Jory added, "I'd better be going." She didn't have anyplace to go, but the walls were closing in on her.

"See you tomorrow?" Melissa sounded hopeful. "Lying around with nothing to do but read and watch TV gets boring."

"Sure." Jory didn't meet her eyes. She left the

hospital, shaking off the scent of medicine and disinfectants. She decided not to go home. Instead she headed for isolated back roads north of the university. She floored the accelerator, and the engine responded. She blasted down the highway, honking her horn, passing startled motorists she thought were going too slowly.

The radio blared, and the noise and the speed soothed her and made her feel in control. Somewhere north of Tarpon Springs a cop caught up with her. He gave her a lecture and a speeding ticket. She shoved it into her glove compartment, knowing that when her mother found out, she'd be in big trouble. "So what?" she said to her reflection in the rearview mirror. "Who cares?" Life was too short to waste. Let her mother say whatever she wanted. Jory really didn't care.

Lyle called her that night and asked her to a movie. She wasn't really interested in going, but her parents were out of town on business and she was lonely. He picked her up and took her to a film she forgot once the credits rolled. "Ice cream?" Lyle asked afterward.

"It's winter."

"Hot fudge takes care of cold nights."

The ice cream parlor was filled with kids from school, and Jory flitted from table to table, laughing and making small talk while Lyle bought hot fudge sundaes.

They sat across from each other in a booth. Jory felt herself relaxing, buoyed by the animated conversation with friends. She swirled her spoon through a blob of warm chocolate. "Tastes good."

"Did you go by the hospital today?"

She felt herself tensing up again. She didn't want to talk about Melissa. "Why are you always asking me about Melissa? Do you like her or something?"

"I know what her family's going through, that's all." His words reminded her that she wasn't a member of the Austin family. "My mother had cancer, Jory. She went through chemo and radiation three years ago. She's been in remission ever since."

His admission startled her and she grew self-conscious, as if Lyle could read her heart and see the hurt. She didn't want anybody to know how much it hurt.

"Cancer's rough on the whole family. It's expensive too," he said.

She wanted to say it was rough on best friends also. "I-I'm glad your mother's all right now, but I don't know what you want me to say about Melissa." She forced a smile and felt foolish.

His amber eyes seemed to be looking inside her. "When my Mom was diagnosed, our whole family went through a special therapy program to help us deal with our feelings about it."

"Sounds good."

"It *was* good, Jory. I learned a lot about myself and how to accept reality. You need to deal with it too."

She shifted her eyes away. "I've dealt with it. I

want Melissa to go on with her life, and I'll help however I can because she's my friend. There's nothing more to say."

"You can talk about how mad you are about it. And how unfair it all is."

He was trying to peel off her shield and she resisted. "Nobody knows how I feel. And I don't want to talk about it with anybody."

"Why? I've been there. I almost lost my mother, Jory."

She shoved the half-eaten sundae aside and stopped smiling. "When you called and invited me to the movie, I said I'd go because I wanted to forget about Melissa and all that's going on. I'm sorry I came."

Lyle stretched out in the booth, jammed his hands into the pockets of his jacket, and studied her. "All right, we won't talk about it. So what did you think of the movie?"

Her mind drew a blank about the plot. "It was all right."

"Okay," Lyle said, "let's try another topic. Any word about your getting into the U of M?"

When had she told him about *that*? "No word yet."

"How about nuclear disarmament, Jory? Want to try that one?"

Anger welled inside her so hot, she felt like throwing something at him. "What's with you? Get off my case!"

Lyle stood abruptly. "Come on, I'll take you home. You're right, this date was a bad idea because you really didn't want to be with me, you just wanted something to keep you busy."

The accusation made her squirm because he was right. "Sorry I'm such a boring date," she flung at him and stalked out to the car.

In the car, Lyle said, "I'm sorry, Jory. I really did want to be with you tonight. I'd like to see you again."

She shook her head, feeling a wave of depression swooping down on her. "It's no good, Lyle. I don't know what I want right now. My head's all mixed up about everything."

In her driveway, he reached out and placed his hand on her shoulder. "If you change your mind, if you need anything . . ."

"I won't," she said, sliding out of the car. She scurried up the walk, not wanting him to follow. She didn't look back, but the warmth where Lyle's hand had rested lingered.

Chapter Ten

On the day of Michael's surgery and Melissa's transplant, Jory skipped school. She sat in the surgical waiting room with Mrs. Austin, who kept an anxious eye on the clock. A woman from her office and a minister had come to wait with her, but it was Jory Melissa's mother talked to most often.

"Why do you suppose it's taking so long?" Jory asked, when they'd been there an hour.

"It could take up to six hours," Mrs. Austin said. "They remove the marrow a pint at a time and spin out the platelets because that's what Melissa needs."

Jory's jaw dropped. "Then it'll be after lunch before we hear anything?"

"I'm afraid so. You don't have to wait the whole time, Jory. You can leave and come back," Mrs. Austin said kindly.

"Oh no. I don't mind. Really. I'd go crazy sitting around at school. Besides, everybody at Lincoln is looking to me for a firsthand report." Jory smiled brightly, knowing that she was as nervous as Mrs. Austin, but able to hide it better. The thought of Michael in an operating room and of some doctor sucking out his bone marrow made her knees go weak. "How's Melissa this morning?"

"She's ready for the transplant. I saw her at six and she was awake and waiting. I'll be checking on her off and on."

"Is she all suppressed?" The question sounded stupid, but Jory didn't know how else to phrase it.

"They've virtually wiped out her immune system. I'm so edgy around her, I don't know what to do. What if some germ slips in despite all the precautions? What if she gets a cold? Or pneumonia? It can happen."

"By then, Michael's bone marrow will be working hard and fighting off the germs," Jory said cheerfully.

Mrs. Austin left to check on Melissa and another hour passed. She returned, saying Melissa was fine but bored. "Did I ever say thank you for all the nice things you've done for Melissa?" She asked.

"I've wanted to do things for her. She's my best friend." Mrs. Austin's gratitude made Jory squirm. "I've wanted to do it for you too, Mrs. Austin. It's meant a lot to me the way you've looked out for me over the years."

"Oh, Jory, I've never minded. I knew right from the start that you and Melissa had a special kind of friendship. Besides, I've always considered you one of my own."

"A-And I've felt like yours too," Jory said, honestly, because she'd never felt closer to Melissa's mother. "You've always made me feel special."

Mrs. Austin smiled. Jory saw deep, tired lines around her eyes and mouth and realized that the pressure must be incredible for her. Both her kids were in the hands of doctors at the same time. "Would you like some coffee? I'll run to the coffee shop for you."

"No. I don't think I could keep it down."

"I know what you mean."

As the noon hour approached, Jory began to think the day would drag on forever. She groped for a topic of conversation to keep her mind busy. "I think you've been so strong through all this, Mrs. Austin."

"Strong? Hardly. I've lost it so many times, I can't count them."

Jory was surprised. "I would have never guessed."

"What choice did I have? I couldn't let Melissa see me scared. And Michael's so angry about the whole thing that I was afraid he'd snap if I didn't keep it together."

"Melissa says that too."

"Why not? He's been a father and brother to her all these years. Now, all this is doubly hard for him."

"Sometimes I get so angry, I want to punch someone out," Jory confessed. "But who? Who's responsible for this?" She eyed the minister and lowered her voice. "I always thought God loved us and wouldn't let anything bad happen to us. Why did He let this happen to Melissa?"

Mrs. Austin studied Jory. "Don't think I haven't asked the same thing. Why *my* daughter?"

"Did you get an answer?" Jory asked, hopefully.

Mrs. Austin stared off into the air. "I've looked for answers everywhere, Jory, and the search isn't over. Rain falls on the just and the unjust, Jory. God is God, we are His creation, and we have no right to question His authority."

Jory bristled because she hated arbitrary authority, hated being pushed around by someone bigger and more powerful than she. Like her own mother. "That's not fair," she muttered.

"God isn't fair. And I don't mean that in a bad way. Fairness implies that we have rights. Do we have the right to tell Him how to run the universe?"

Jory furrowed her brow. "Maybe not."

"Then why should we have the right to tell Him how to order our lives?"

"But what did Melissa ever do to deserve cancer?"

"Nothing. I suppose that's where the great mystery lies. People don't get what they deserve— good or bad. Life isn't always so logical."

"The rain falling on the just and unjust?" Jory asked.

"Yes, but regardless, we still have one very real thing going for us. We have hope, and I think that's what separates us from the rest of creation. We get to hold on to hope . . . hope for things not seen."

Jory was moved by Mrs. Austin's faith and she wondered if she'd ever feel that way herself. Would she ever come to accept gracefully what she couldn't understand or change? "All I want is for Melissa to get well and everything to be normal again. When I think of all the plans she's made—of her dream to be a lawyer and all . . ."

"Melissa is single-minded. And she's like a bulldog. Once she latches onto something, she doesn't let go."

"That's good, don't you think? I mean, if she's a fighter, it's got to count in her favor."

"That's what her doctors tell me." Mrs. Austin patted Jory's hand absently. "I'm glad you stopped wearing that blue fingernail polish. You have pretty hands."

Jory glanced at her unpolished nails, unable to remember the last time she had done them. "Just one of my phases." How silly that period of Jory's life seemed to her now—the strange hairdos and outlandish clothes. She'd done it merely to get a rise out of her mother. It had worked, yet nothing was different between them. They were still butting heads and arguing over everything. Jory sighed, shaking off the direction of her thoughts. There were too many other, more important things to think about now. Like Melissa, and Michael, in surgery.

The door swung open and Michael's surgeon

entered. Jory crowded near Mrs. Austin, determined to hear his report.

"Michael did fine. He's young and strong and came through like a champ. He's in recovery now, but we'll send him to his room once his vital signs stabilize." The physician took Mrs. Austin's hand. "We removed six pints of marrow through two holes in his backside. He'll be sore for a few days, but that's the worst of it for your son."

"And Melissa?"

"We've sent the bags to isolation."

Jory noticed that Mrs. Austin's hands were shaking. "I'd better go on up . . ."

The doctor started to leave, then turned. "It's a precious gift your son has given his sister."

"I know," Mrs. Austin said. "He's given her a second chance at life." The doctor left, and the minister and Mrs. Austin's friend gathered closer. Mrs. Austin told them, "Thank you for coming. Both of you." Then confusion clouded her face.

Jory asked, "What's wrong?"

"Suddenly, I don't know what to do. . . . I mean, Michael's in recovery and Melissa's waiting for me. I want to be with both of them. But there's only one of me."

Jory said, "Michael would want you to go to Melissa."

"Yes. Of course, you're right." Mrs. Austin headed for the elevators for the ride up to the isolation ward.

"Tell her I'll buy her a five-pound box of chocolates," Jory called as the elevator doors closed behind Mrs. Austin. Alone in the roomful of strangers, Jory picked up her purse and started for the elevators too. She punched the button for the ground floor when an idea struck. She could wait in Michael's room until he came down from recovery. Then she could see with her own eyes that he was fine.

Jory held her breath as she slipped inside the private room where Michael was already asleep. Jory stepped close to the bed. The hollows below his eyes appeared darkened and bruised, showing how stressful the surgery had been on his body. She listened to the soft sounds of his breathing. She fussed over the sheet, pulling it closer to his neck, and let her hand linger on his shoulder, tentatively, careful not to wake him.

His black hair fell over his forehead and she gently brushed it aside, allowing herself the luxury of touching him. He didn't stir and Jory grew bolder. She stroked his cheek and felt the rough stubble of his beard. She placed her palm along the length of his face and her heart pounded. How long had she dreamed of touching him like this? "Michael . . ." she whispered.

She remembered all the times he'd teased her and ignored her. She was a kid—Melissa's "little rich friend." It didn't matter. Nothing mattered but the love she felt that made her pulse throb and her heart ache.

"Prince Charming's asleep," she murmured, amused by this ironic turn of events. Jory glanced

around the room. They were alone. Closed blinds
held off twilight, and in the soft arms of shadow Jory
leaned forward. With measured purpose, she
traced the outline of his lips with her fingertips,
then bent and kissed him longingly on the mouth.

Only immediate family members were allowed
to see Melissa for the first week. It infuriated Jory
to have to get information from the nurses' station
or from Mrs. Austin. "Nothing yet," Melissa's
mother told her over the phone when Jory called.
"So far nothing's happening with the transplant."

Jory worked up her courage to visit Michael,
who was recovering but still in a lot of discomfort. "I
feel sixty years old," he grumbled. "I can't even
stand up straight."

A nurse clucked over him and assured him the
pain would pass. "Here. I brought you a present,"
Jory said, placing a book about ballooning on his
bed after the nurse had left.

He picked it up and flipped through beautiful
color photographs of earth taken from hot-air balloons. "Geez, Jory, this book must have cost fifty
bucks."

His comment stung, but she ignored it. "It was
on the discount table and I thought it would get you
close to the sky until you felt like doing the real
thing again."

He closed the book. "Thanks, but I don't know
if I'll ever go back up. It all seems so pointless now."

She wanted to protest, but what right did she

have to encourage him? "Will you be out soon?" She asked.

"Not soon enough. Maybe tomorrow. I went up to see Melissa, though."

"How's she doing?"

"Not much change. It makes me mad. I thought for sure they'd be able to tell something by now."

"It's not been that long . . ." Jory said, letting the sentence trail when Michael glared at her. She hated it whenever she said silly, innocuous things. And she hated it when Michael looked at her like she was a child. She remembered kissing him and her cheeks flushed.

"I hate this place," Michael said through clenched teeth. "I feel like I'm in a cage."

Jory shifted from foot to foot, understanding exactly what he meant. She opened her mouth to speak, but Mrs. Austin came through the door. She looked pale, like she hadn't slept in a week.

Michael sat straight up in his bed and blanched. "Man, that hurt," he mumbled. He reached out to his mother. "What's wrong, Mom?"

Jory stepped aside, trying to make herself unobtrusive. Cold fear knotted her stomach, because she could tell something was wrong. Very wrong. "Melissa has a fever," Mrs. Austin said, taking Michael's hand. "She's sick, Michael. And it's either an infection or the first signs of rejection."

Chapter Eleven

~~~~

"Melissa needs blood. Will you help me?" Jory spoke to Lyle, who was sitting at a table in the school library with books and papers spread out in front of him.

"I'll give blood," he said.

Jory fidgeted. "She needs lots of blood. I've asked permission from the principal to organize a blood drive for her. But I need help." Lyle was watching her so intently that she almost turned and ran off. "You said to come to you if I ever needed anything," she said, almost accusingly. "Will you help, or not?"

Under the table he shoved back the chair across from him with his foot. "Sit down." Jory sat on the edge, tapping her foot impatiently. "What's happened?" Lyle asked.

"I'm not sure. Mrs. Austin just said that she needs blood. She's getting it through the blood bank, but they need to replenish what Melissa uses. I figured it was something I could help with. There're plenty of kids at school who would like to do something. Everyone asks about Melissa. I know people care."

Lyle hunched forward, wrinkling his brow and

nodding thoughtfully. "We could do more than organize a blood drive."

"What do you mean?"

"I told you that my mom had cancer. It almost wiped us out financially. I'll bet the Austins are hurting for money by now too. Can you guess how much all this must be costing them?"

Jory shook her head, but recalled that Melissa often worried about money and what would happen when her mom's insurance ran out. What Lyle was saying made sense. She wished she'd thought of it. "What have you got in mind?"

"A carnival here at the school. Something that the whole community can come to. We'll call it Melissa Austin Day—"

"—and we'll charge a donation of blood for admission!" Jory cried, catching on to his idea.

Lyle grinned. "Two bucks if you're squeamish."

"We can have the newspaper write it up. Maybe some radio stations will give us some time on the air to talk about it. There are lots of stores in this area. We could ask them for merchandise and raffle it off," Jory rambled on, her mind racing with ideas. "We can charge for games of chance. Different clubs here at school can man booths, and all of the proceeds will go toward Melissa's hospital bills. Of course, we'll take straight donations too. We'll have to set up a special account at a bank. . . ."

By now, Jory was bursting. "It's a great idea, Lyle. You and I will be the main committee. Let me get some of the faculty to help too. I know Mrs. Watson will. Melissa's always been her favorite." Jory scrambled for her notebook and began jotting notes furiously. "If we get right on it, I'll bet we could get it together in two weeks. That's right before Gasparilla. Maybe we could even have a float in the parade . . ."

"Whoa," Lyle cautioned with a laugh. "Boy when you catch on to something, you go all out."

Jory shrugged sheepishly. "Okay. I got carried away. No float. But the carnival is perfect and we can use a pirate theme." She tapped her lips with the end of her pencil. "My parents are wired to everybody in this city. They could help get some nice donations."

"Would they?"

Jory thought back to her party and wondered the same thing. "Sure," she said, with a confidence she didn't feel. "A few things anyway."

Lyle crossed his arms and studied her. "You're really into this idea, aren't you?"

Jory looked straight at him. "Last summer, I promised Melissa that we'd have the best senior year ever. But she got sick again and I feel like I haven't followed through on my promise. This will make up for it."

"You're a great friend, Jory."

She blushed and stood up quickly. "Geez, I've got a million things to do. Let me get started and I'll call you tonight. And thanks, Lyle. I mean it. It's a great plan, and Melissa's family needs it."

Lyle caught her hand and squeezed it. "It's not just for Melissa, Jory. It's for you too."

She felt her breath catch in her throat as she stared into his amber eyes. "Then thanks from both of us," she said and skittered away.

"That'll be one pint of blood. Step into the bloodmobile behind me." Jory flashed a flirtatious smile at the two senior boys waiting to donate blood and get into the carnival.

"I wouldn't do this for just anyone, Delaney," one of them said.

"Don't give me some line about helping Melissa," Jory teased. "You just want the chance to dunk the principal in the water tank at the baseball toss."

The boy grinned. "Hey, now that sounds like fun!"

The boys entered an enormous blue-and-white vehicle, and Jory stacked a pile of dollar bills from the many who'd paid cash to get into the carnival.

"How's it going?" Lyle asked as he came up to her.

"Business couldn't be better. How's it going on your end?"

"The water balloon throw was wet." He shook drops of water from his hair. "And two freshmen won the egg toss."

"When do we raffle off the weekend for two at the beach?"

"After lunch. It was great of your parents to

persuade that resort to make the offer. Are they here?"

Jory dropped her eyes and her smile faded a bit. She thought back to her mother's reluctance to help. "It's not that we don't approve of what you're doing, Jory," Mrs. Delaney had said. "We'd like to help, but . . ."

Jory had gotten angry. "All you have to do is *ask*, Mother."

Jory told Lyle, "They have other plans and won't get by. But who cares? We're doing a booming business."

Lyle closed the cash box and said, "Why don't you take a break and walk around and see the sights with me?"

"But we need someone to man the entrance."

Lyle whistled shrilly and three players Jory recognized from the basketball team jogged over. "Let Larry, Curly, and Moe fill in for a while," he joked. "Can you dudes handle it?"

The guys razzed one another, but sat dutifully at the table. Jory explained the procedure to them and then she and Lyle made their way through the crowds. He took her hand. "Wouldn't want you to get lost."

"I'm a big girl," she said, but she didn't pull away.

Blue sky blended with warm sunshine. The smell of hot buttered popcorn and candied apples hung in the air. Jory inhaled. "We got lucky. February can turn mean, but today's gorgeous."

"I special-ordered it," Lyle said. He stopped in front of a booth. "Want to try your luck knocking down the bottles?"

"You don't think I can do it, do you?"

He shook his head. "It's a game of skill. Girls aren't any good at games of skill."

"Watch this, buster." Jory plopped down a dollar, and the attendant, whom she recognized from her Spanish class, handed her four baseballs. Two minutes later, every stack of bottles lay in a heap.

Lyle raised his hands in surrender. "I take it back. You're terrific."

"And don't you forget it."

He reached out and touched her cheek. "How can I?"

Jory felt flustered, suddenly ill at ease. She glanced away. "What's that long line for over there?"

Lyle followed her pointing finger. "That's the cheerleaders' booth. They're selling kisses for a buck, and making a fortune too."

"Humph," Jory said and flounced over to the booth. She watched a line of guys putting up their money and being kissed. Lyle eased behind her. "They certainly get into their work," Jory said, arching her eyebrow. "Especially Shirley Vaughan. Look at her. If she gets any closer we may have to hire a surgical team to extract her."

Lyle placed his hands on her shoulders and she felt the length of him against her back. It was comforting and she didn't want to move. She leaned into him ever so slightly. His fingers tightened gently.

"Hey, Delaney!" A guy from the line yelled. "I'll give you *two* bucks if you'll kiss me."

She started to refuse, but then an impish grin lit her face. "Make it three."

The kid moaned. "Geez, the things I do for love."

He shouldered his way through the line. As Jory took her place in the booth, she flashed Shirley a smile. The cheerleader tossed her head and stepped aside. Jory kissed the boy and attempted to leave, despite a chorus of cheers for her to stay. "Drop it, fellas," she called. "This was a one time only." Suddenly, Lyle stepped forward and slapped down five dollars.

Startled, she stared and whispered, "Lyle, don't be silly, we're on the committee together."

"Every penny counts." he told her, leaning forward. "Besides, it's not for me. It's for Melissa."

Someone overheard him and began to chant, "Go for it, Lyle!"

Jory's pulse fluttered as Lyle's hands came up and cupped her chin. She caught her breath as his lips came down on hers, very soft and very sweet.

"Are you mad at me?"

Lyle's question and boyish grin almost caused Jory to forget that she was annoyed with him. "That was a dirty trick you played on me this afternoon."

"What trick? I paid five bucks for a kiss." She turned her head, determined to stay miffed, but he dipped into her line of vision. "It's my money and it was worth it."

She warmed her hands on a mug of hot chocolate and watched as several faculty members counted the receipts for the day on the far side of the gym. "Fifty people were watching and it was embarrassing."

"I could arrange a private performance."

Jory fumbled with her cup, confused. Lyle was getting too personal and she didn't want that. This day was for Melissa. The thought of Melissa made her sober. "I called the hospital," she told him, ignoring his offer. "Mrs. Austin says that Melissa's got a rash now and they're working on the assumption that she's rejecting Michael's bone marrow."

Lyle eased beside her in the bleachers. "I'm sorry. But maybe the tide will turn. I've done some reading. Rejection can reverse itself."

Jory shrugged. "Sometimes I feel that we're all on a big merry-go-round and we can't get off."

"Where's Little Miss Optimism?"

"Going down for the count," Jory confessed with a tired sigh.

"We did great today," Lyle said, enthusiastically. "We got gallons of blood and raised a ton of money."

"It *was* a good day, huh?" Jory felt lifted by his good humor and offered a tired smile. "Mrs. Austin was really touched. When I told her what we were planning on doing, I thought she'd break down and cry."

"You'll have to give her a final tally tomorrow. Maybe things will be looking better all the way around by then."

"Maybe so." Jory leaned on the bleacher. "I'm wiped out," she confessed.

"Look, I'll go over and get a ballpark figure from the principal and then take you home. You can call her first thing tomorrow."

Jory watched him cross the gym floor and wondered where he'd gotten his energy. Her thoughts returned to Melissa lying in her hospital room, fighting for her life. She thought of Michael too. Michael, whose bone marrow was to have given his sister a second chance at life. Jory wanted to be with them both.

Lyle returned, his brow knitted thoughtfully. "What's up? Do they need a Brinks truck to haul it away?"

"We got some checks in donations," Lyle said. "From people who didn't come."

"That's good, although this afternoon it seemed like half of Tampa showed up."

Lyle handed her a check. She saw the amount—five thousand dollars—and whistled. Then she saw the signature and gasped. The check was signed by her mother.

Chapter Twelve

~~~

"Why did you do it, Mother?" Jory impatiently shifted from foot to foot in her parent's study, a room painted forest green and accented with brass and ferns.

The desk lamp cast shadows on the wall as her mother worked on real estate contracts at her antique desk. "Do what, Jory?"

"I saw the check for Melissa. It shocked me that you would donate so much money to her family. Why didn't you tell me you were going to do that?"

Mrs. Delaney put down her pen and removed her glasses. "I'm not insensitive, Jory. I know how much Melissa means to you and I feel very sorry for her family and what they must be going through."

"It's been going on for a long time. Why are you suddenly so concerned?" Jory knew she was being rude, but she didn't care.

"I've never seen you so involved in anything before," her mother countered. "I was impressed."

"So you were rewarding *me*? A whole bunch of people worked to make this thing happen, you know." Jory wanted to tell her about Lyle, because without him, she would have never pulled it off.

"That's not it. Stop being so defensive. But Jory, you must admit that you put very little effort into things that you do. I simply think you did an excellent job on this carnival for your friend. I heard it talked about on the radio, and the article in the newspaper was good too."

"If you were so impressed, then why didn't you and Daddy stop by?"

"Your father's flown down to the islands on business and I was swamped with desk work and couldn't get away." Mrs. Delaney paused. "How did it go? Did you raise lots of money?"

"Yes. But Melissa's not doing so well. They think she might be rejecting the transplant."

"That's too bad. Really, I'm sorry."

"She knew that was a possibility when she checked in to the hospital. But she had the procedure done anyway. Her mother thought she was mature enough to make the decision herself."

"That is a big decision for such a young girl. . . ." Mrs. Delaney shifted and glanced at her watch. "You should go to bed and get some rest."

Jory felt like screaming. How could her mother bounce so easily between caring and indifference? "I'm tired, but I'm not sleepy," she said, plopping onto a sofa.

"That happens to me sometimes," Mrs. Delaney swiveled in her chair to face Jory. "Maybe you'd like some hot tea?"

"I had hot chocolate already." Jory plucked at a decorator pillow.

"What is it, Jory? What do you want?" Her tone was kind, a bit imploring.

Jory didn't know exactly. Her antagonism waned and she felt restless and unsettled. "I-I want to thank you for the money," she said. "It was a big donation and I know it will help the Austins."

Mrs. Delaney heaved a sigh and pressed her eyelids with her fingers. "I honestly feel sorry for that family. I can't imagine how I'd handle it if it were you."

The remark caught Jory off guard. It had never occurred to her that her mother ever thought about her in any way except as someone to order around. "I don't know how I'd handle it if it were me either."

"I'm glad it isn't you." Her mother's face was bathed in lamplight, and for a moment, Jory thought she saw her eyes glistening.

She recalled all the arguments they'd had over the past months and realized that these were the first gentle words they'd shared in ages. She remembered another scene. One of Mrs. Austin cradling Melissa beside their Christmas tree. She couldn't remember the last time her mother had held her like that. "Well, I guess I'll go to my room." She struggled to her feet, suddenly exhausted.

She got as far as the door before her mother said, "Uh, Jory. There is one thing." Jory tensed. She should have known their moment of peaceful coexistence wouldn't last. "I appreciate the way you've stuck to your bargain about going to all the engagements I've arranged over these past months."

"A deal's a deal."

"I know it hasn't been exactly fun to go out on arranged dates."

"I knew it was important to you and Dad."

"Well, I'm releasing you from that commitment. There's one I set up months ago for the first of March that I'd really appreciate if you'd keep, but after that, you don't ever have to go to something I've arranged if you don't want to."

Jory turned, open-mouthed. "I don't?"

"You don't."

"Gee, Mom—thanks. Really, I mean, thanks a *lot*."

Mrs. Delaney shrugged. "Don't act like you've just been released from prison. I know sometimes it seems that all we ever do is fight. That we always seem to be working at cross purposes. But, Jory, all I've ever wanted for you was the best from life."

Jory's eyes flew up to her mother's. "We've just never been able to agree on what was 'the best.'"

"No, I guess not."

The tick of the antique wall clock was the only sound to break the silence between them. Jory had an overwhelming urge to slip into her mother's arms and rest her head against her. She didn't move. "Well, good night," she finally said, clearing her throat.

"Good night, Jory," Mrs. Delaney said. "Please keep me posted on Melissa's progress."

"I will." Jory slipped into the hall and up the stairs feeling quite alone.

For reasons she didn't understand, Jory spent every night of the next week studying. She was almost finished with an English term paper on Saturday night, when Lyle called. "Want to hit a party with me?" he asked.

She stretched and eyed the paper. "Tell me more."

"Some of the guys are checking out a big bash in the woods north of the university. A couple of them are planning on going to USF next fall, and a few of the fraternities are having a free-for-all out there tonight. I'd like you to come with me."

Jory was tempted. "Gee, Lyle, I don't know . . . I've got this paper due Monday." She toyed with her pen, and inspiration struck. "Tell you what. Give me directions, and I'll meet you out there when I'm finished."

"You're on." She heard the smile in his voice over the phone. She hung up and wondered why she'd agreed. She loved parties, but it was more than that. She'd wanted to be with Lyle. "That's stupid!" she said aloud, flipping through the book to find her place and get back to work. Lyle Vargas was just a nice guy who was sensitive and understanding about her friendship with Melissa. That was all. For Jory there was only Michael. Always and forever. Only Michael.

A few hours later, Jory parked her car and followed the sounds of music to a clearing in the pine trees. The moon was full, its light filtering through the trees, and the night air was cool and crisp. Auxiliary floodlights, fed by a portable generator, had been set up in a haphazard circle. Vehicles were scattered everywhere, and people danced, some on the hoods of the cars.

Her eyes darted about nervously. She didn't recognize a soul of the college crowd, most of whom were drinking. She had almost talked herself into leaving when Lyle called to her. "It's a little crazy around here, but I'm glad you came," he said.

She flashed him a perky smile. "You know me, just a party girl at heart."

Lyle eyed her, shaking his head. "Why do you keep pushing that image of yourself? You're far more than that, Jory."

"Never!"

"Yeah you are. I know you want everybody to think you're only running around looking for a good time, but you're not that way at all. Look at how much you do for Melissa."

"Cripes, Lyle, you make me sound like Mother Teresa." Jory felt silly listening to him sing her praises. Although she'd once wanted to change her image from a good-time girl, she didn't want anything to interfere with her promises to Melissa right now. She slid out of his grasp. "So where's the gang?"

"Skip and Tommy are putting the moves on some girls. I've just been hanging back waiting for you."

"So here I am," she said brightly. "Why don't we dance?"

"Can we wait for something slow?"

She watched several couples whirl in frenzied motion. "Doesn't look like there will be anything slow coming on the pipes for a long time. Come on, don't be a party pooper. I want to have *fun*!"

Lyle danced with her, and in minutes Jory was caught up in music and motion. She welcomed the opportunity to clear her mind, to relax and let loose. When something slow did blare over the speakers, she sighed. Slow meant thinking and talking, and right now Jory didn't want to do either. Lyle pulled her to him, locking his hands behind the small of her back. "This is much better," he said, catching his breath and resting his chin on top of her head.

The air was cool on her warm skin and Lyle was near and his arms were holding her and he smelled of warmth and woodsy cologne. It would be so easy to nestle against him, to bury her face in his chest and float in his arms. "I'm thirsty," she said, holding herself away from him. "Do they have sodas, or is beer the only thing to drink?"

Lyle stopped dancing but didn't release her. "Look at me." She tipped her head upward. "What's wrong, Jory?"

"Nothing's wrong." She offered a brilliant smile. "Can't I be thirsty?"

"Whenever you smile like that it means, 'Don't get too close.' Why can't you talk to me, Jory? I've been there."

"Been where? And I'm so sorry my smile bothers you." Why did he always have to dig inside her? Why couldn't he just leave her alone and have a good time?

She squirmed out of his arms and walked to the edge of the circle of light. He followed. "Look, Lyle, maybe I shouldn't have come. You want to be serious and I want to party. Everybody accepts me just the way I am, Lyle, except you." *And my mother and Melissa*, she thought. "Why can't everybody just leave me alone and let me live my own life?"

"Your best friend is *dying*, Jory. You can't stand by and watch it happen and not have it tear your guts out. *Talk* to me. I can help."

"She's not dying!" Jory yelled. "She's sick and she's having problems with her cure, but she's not going to die." Pressure began to build in her chest as she spoke.

"It isn't your fault that Melissa got sick and you didn't," Lyle said.

"That's stupid," she hissed. "That's never crossed my mind." The tightness in her chest increased and she wanted to bolt. Lyle reached for her, but she shoved him away. "Leave me alone. I mean it. Melissa's going to make it."

"But what if she doesn't? What will you do?"

"I'll be just fine with all my *real* friends around me. Up 'til now, you've been a good friend, but . . ."

He lifted his hands to her face and ran his thumbs along the sides of her cheeks, making her shiver. "I don't want to be your buddy, Jory. I don't want to be just another one of the guys you run around partying with."

Lyle's words had hurt and she wanted to hurt him back. "Let me be real honest with you, Lyle, all right? The only guy I've ever been crazy about is Michael Austin. I've felt that way for years, and even though I date other guys, no one's ever been able to change my mind about him."

Lyle said nothing, but his eyes looked dark and hurt. Jory wished she could take it all back. Lyle had been good to her and kind to Melissa. He said, "In other words, 'Buzz off, Lyle.' Is that the bottom line?"

She raised her chin. "You got it."

"Thanks for being honest, Jory. You get your wish. I won't bother you anymore. You drove yourself here, I guess you can drive yourself home." He walked away and quickly disappeared into the clusters of people.

Alone in the moonlight, Jory swallowed a lump of hot tears. She didn't care. Let him go! She sniffed and ran her fingers through her hair, damp at the temples from anxiety. She glanced about, not sure what to do or where to go.

She heard a familiar voice call her name from across the clearing and her stomach did a somersault. She turned to see Michael Austin coming toward her.

Chapter Thirteen

Michael wore a cockeyed grin as he approached her, weaving slightly as he walked. Jory knew instantly that he'd been drinking. "Hey, Jory. What're you doin' here?"

He'd greeted her like a long-lost friend and she realized exactly how drunk he had to be. Michael had rarely been very friendly to her, especially over the past few months. "Looking for a good time," she told him gaily.

"Then you've come to the right place," Michael said, looping his arm over her shoulders. "We're all having a real good time."

All thoughts of Lyle and their argument fled. "It looks like you've gotten a head start, Michael. How long have you been here?"

He attempted to read his watch. "Hands look fuzzy," he said, tapping the face. "Gotta get the thing fixed."

"Are you . . . uh . . . with somebody, Michael?" Jory asked.

He leaned into her and scratched his head, as if trying to remember. "Just some guys."

Jory was relieved. She felt euphoric over his being nice to her and she didn't want to share him, even if he was smashed and wouldn't remember a thing in the morning. "Why don't we sit down?" she asked.

"In a minute. First, I need to get a beer."

"Don't you think you've had enough beers?"

It was the wrong thing to say. "I know when I've had enough," he said abruptly.

Anxious not to lose him, Jory flashed him one of her most fabulous smiles. "Of course. So why don't I sit here on the car and wait for you?"

"Works for me," he said with a wave of his hand.

She watched him thread through the crowd toward an area with two stainless steel beer kegs and a washtub of other drinks. She knew that it wasn't smart for him to be drinking so much, but she also knew what he'd been through since Melissa's illness began. He deserved to blow off some steam.

A guy came toward her and Jory stiffened, willing Michael to return. "You a friend of Austin's?" He asked.

Jory hesitated. "Yes."

"Me too. I've been trying to get him out of here for an hour. But he won't go."

"He doesn't do this sort of thing often," she said, feeling a need to defend Michael.

"I know. You think you can get his car keys from him and get him home? He's too far gone to drive, and I'm not much better off myself."

Slightly ashamed that she hadn't thought of it herself, Jory asked, "Where are they?"

"In the pocket of the windbreaker he's wearing."

"What about you? How will you get home?"

The guy glanced behind him toward a blond-haired girl waiting patiently beside a red car. "I have a ride."

"Oh . . . yeah, sure. Don't worry, I'll get Michael home."

The guy left with the girl and Jory waited, holding her breath, until Michael wove his way back through the crowd. He dropped a cola in her lap and took a long swallow from a plastic mug. Jory realized that in spite of all he'd had to drink, he hadn't forgotten that she was too young for beer. She was still just a kid to him. She stood and slipped snugly beneath his arm. "So what now?"

Michael scanned the party scene. "I don't know . . ."

"We could dance," she said, deftly sliding her free hand into his pocket and taking the keys to his truck.

"We could."

She slipped the keys into the pocket of her hooded sweatshirt, where she kept her own. She remembered that it was only a week after his surgery and asked, "You are recovered, aren't you? I mean, the last time I saw you, you couldn't even stand up straight."

"See what a few beers can accomplish?" he said. "Naw, I'm all better, Jory. Fit and perfectly healthy."

She thought she detected sarcasm in his voice and didn't want to be the one to bring him back to reality. Not when she knew firsthand how much reality hurt. Michael put his cup on the hood of the car and took the cola from Jory's hand. "Are we gonna dance or not?"

She went to his arms without a word. Slow music pulsed through the woods, throbbing with words of broken promises and lost love. She felt nervous, being so close to him, as if she might wake and discover it was all a dream. He draped his wrists over her shoulders and toyed with the back of her hair. He touched his forehead to hers and she closed her eyes, held her breath, and hoped the music would never stop.

"Let's get out of here," Michael said, his voice low and soft.

Her eyes flew open and her mouth went dry. "All right."

She watched him as he fumbled for his keys, feeling guilty because she knew they were safe inside her pocket. "What's wrong?"

"Can't find my keys. Hell, I just had them . . ."

"No problem." Jory displayed a dazzling smile and hooked her arm through his. "I've got my car."

"But my truck . . . and my buddy . . ."

"Who's going to miss you in this crowd? And so what if your truck sits here all night? You can get it tomorrow." She was glad he couldn't follow her logic because she had none. She had only her smile and bravado.

Michael shook his head, as if to clear it, but didn't protest as she led him to where she'd parked. "Ah, you brought your lean, mean machine," Michael said when he saw her convertible.

"Put the top down," he ordered. "I want to ride with the wind in my face."

She lowered the roof and maneuvered the car through the maze of other vehicles. At the road, she asked, "Why don't we just drive? I know these back roads like the palm of my hand." She didn't want him to decide he had to go home. She just wanted to prolong the night spending time with him.

"Suits me," Michael said, scooting down into the bucket seat and crossing his arms.

Jory drove cautiously. Fields stretched on either side of the two lanes and there wasn't another car in sight.

"Is this the best it can do?" Michael asked.

"What do you mean?"

"Is this as fast as this baby can go? I want to go fast, Jory. Real fast."

She stared over at him. His face was pale in the moonlight, his eyes dark hollows. "Buckle up and hang on," she said, remembering the last time she'd blasted down these roads and a cop had stopped her. She reached out and turned up the radio full blast, gunned the engine, and floored the accelerator. The car responded instantly, and she watched the speedometer needle climb from the fifties through the sixties and into the seventies. The road beckoned like a long white river. The wind stung her face. Fence posts and telephone poles streaked by in a blur. Her exhilaration and sense of recklessness rose until she felt at one with the wind and the moon and the night.

Jory tipped her head back and laughed. The sound seemed to bounce off the stars. She looked toward Michael. Her heart almost stopped. Michael was sitting on the top edge of the front seat, with one arm grasping the seat belt and the other raised above his head. The wind whipped his hair.

"Michael, no!" She pumped the brake, jolting the speeding car, causing it to career. It took all her skill to keep it on the road. She managed to slow down and coasted along the shoulder of the highway, where the vehicle finally rolled to a halt. The screaming radio shattered the stillness. She turned it off so violently that the knob broke.

Lazily, Michael slid downward into the seat cushion, as if nothing had happened. "Why'd you stop? I was having fun."

"You scared me to death! Are you trying to get killed?"

"I just wanted to feel what it was like . . ."

"Then go to Busch Gardens and take a ride on the roller coaster!" Jory's whole body quivered. "What's the matter with you?"

Michael shrugged his shoulders indifferently. "Don't get so bent out of shape. It was a little like riding in my balloon, only faster."

"But there's no basket to hold you in," she said, gritting her teeth.

He stared at her, his eyes calm in the moon-light. "I know."

The words sent a chill through her, more intense than the fear. She sucked in a long, shuttering breath. "Why don't we try it again," she said. "This time I'll keep the speed down and would you please keep your seat?"

"You don't have to get pushy," Michael said, grinning.

Her hands trembled, but she returned a shaky smile. "I'll try not to act so bossy the next time my passenger almost climbs out of my car when I'm doing seventy." She put the car into gear and inched out onto the highway. She drove more slowly, glancing at Michael every few minutes. He was brooding now, quiet and pensive. She wanted to touch him, chase away the darkness that was engulfing him.

"I know someplace I could show you," Jory said brightly, with an edge of mystery. "It's a great place and I know you'll love it."

He only shrugged, so she drove until she came upon a dirt road, where she turned off and followed the trail that was sheltered by overhanging trees. She came to a clearing where moss hung from trees and a stream gurgled in the woods. Jory cut the engine, and night noises filled up the silence.

Michael looked around. "Where are we?"

"A place Melissa showed me." Jory wondered if she should have told him because he might want to know how Melissa had discovered it.

Instead, he took a deep breath and closed his eyes. The sweet scent of orange blossoms and night-blooming jasmine drifted on an occasional breeze. "I like it," he said and she relaxed. "I wish I had a beer," he told her. "The wind and the ride seem to have sobered me up."

"What's wrong with that? Now you can see the hands on your watch, I'll bet."

"Because sober isn't where I want to be. Because when I'm sober I know the truth."

The look of pain that crossed his face etched a line across Jory's heart. "What truth, Michael?"

"That my sister's dying. And it's all my fault."

Chapter Fourteen

His words stunned her. It took a moment before she found her voice. "Michael, that's not true! How can you even think that?"

"Because it is true. Who'd she get that lousy bone marrow from? Who told her it was 'primo stuff'? It isn't first-rate after all, Jory. It's killing her."

"Michael, it isn't your fault. Melissa would never think that. You were the best donor—" she paused, "the *only* donor. Without you, she had no hope."

"And with me, she got a one-way ticket to doom." A bitter frown formed on his mouth. "She trusted me . . ." Michael opened the car door and walked away. Jory scrambled after him, anxious and fearful.

At the stream, he stooped and gathered a handful of pebbles and began to bounce them into the water. "The first time she was in the hospital, I thought I'd go nuts." A pebble plopped, sent rings through the moonlit water, and sank. "Every day, I'd go in and see what the chemo was doing to her. It invaded her, turned her inside out, and made her hurt so bad. All the doctors said was 'It's normal. It's

115

always this way.' I hated those doctors, and I hated what their 'cure' was doing to her."

He'd said the word *cure* like it was dirty.

"But the chemo did help," Jory told him. "It put her into remission, and she went home and back to school."

Michael depleted his supply of rocks and stared out across the stream. "Yeah, she did. I thought, 'It's over. A nasty business, but all behind us now.'"

"But she relapsed," Jory said, reliving her own reaction to the news.

"It was like a bad joke. Like Lucy holding the football for Charlie Brown. You know, every time she promises to keep it upright for him to kick, and every time he gets suckered in and runs to kick it."

"And Lucy jerks it away," Jory finished.

"That's the way the doctors were. 'So sorry, Melissa. But we have this other cure. Want to go for it?'" He mimicked Dr. Rowan's voice. "And I said, 'Go for it, Melissa. You can have my bone marrow, and afterward you'll be cured.'"

Jory searched for words of assurance. Anything that would make him stop blaming himself. "Sometimes I feel like I'm responsible too, Michael. I wanted her to have the transplant. I encouraged her too."

"Well we were both wrong, weren't we?" His tone was bitter.

"But the odds were so bad without it," Jory rationalized, not sure she was addressing Michael at all.

"That's the way it is with doctors," he interrupted. "They're always quoting the odds. Makes me wonder why they don't play the horses and leave people alone."

An icy lump settled in Jory's stomach. Hesitantly, she reached out and touched his arm. "It's going to work, Michael. I know it is. Melissa is seventeen years old and she's pretty and smart and she has everything going for her. W-we just have to have h-hope . . ."

Her voice broke and Michael gave her a piercing look. "Come back to the car," he said gently, taking her hand. She followed, fighting for composure. She couldn't lose it in front of Michael. Mature girls don't cry, she reminded herself as they walked.

At the car, Michael climbed into the backseat, nestled into a corner, and pulled Jory next to him. He placed her head against his chest and stroked her hair. She settled into his embrace and listened to his heart, its rhythm calm and soothing.

His mouth pressed against her temple. "It's okay, Jory. Take it easy. I didn't mean to get so morose. I'm sorry." She couldn't move, didn't want to move. "I just feel so helpless," he whispered. "I thought my bone marrow would stop it. I thought that after the operation, she'd wake up the next day and smile and get up out of her hospital bed and be well. Like a miracle would happen and Melissa would be healthy again." His voice sounded thick and she was afraid to look into his eyes in case there were tears in them.

"It might happen yet," Jory said, her voice small and hopeful. "Melissa's a fighter and it's worked for others. Don't give up, Michael. Please." She looked up at him finally. She wanted to make him stop hurting, wanted to make everything all right again. His mouth was but inches away. She stretched upward and kissed him.

This time he was not asleep and his lips moved beneath hers, hesitantly at first, then more urgently. His arms tightened and his hands began to move down the length of her back, urging her against him. She pressed into him, feeling energy and fire along the hardness of his body.

She shifted, brought her arms up around his neck and stroked his hair. His mouth left hers and began to travel, in frantic little trails over her hair, her face, her throat. She gasped, tugging him closer, wishing she could sink into him. He caught his fingers in the sides of her hair and found her mouth again.

For Jory, time stood still and six years of frustrated yearning erupted like a volcano. Her head spun and every nerve in her body tingled. Her blood sizzled. The scent of jasmine drenched the air, and the taste of Michael blotted out reason and doubt. His hands found her bare skin, making her shiver. She poured herself into the kiss, giving, giving . . .

Without warning, Michael broke away. The night air chilled her face and she shifted uneasily. The tilting world slowly righted itself. He was staring at her, his eyes unblinking, his breath coming in gulps. She drew back, confused and disoriented.

"Jory, I . . ." His voice shook.

"Don't," she said, reality rushing over her like cold water. She tugged her clothing into place with numb and clumsy fingers.

"Jory, I'm sorry. My God . . . what almost happened. What I almost did to you."

She covered her embarrassment with nonchalance, trying to sound sophisticated. "What's the big deal? You think some guy's never tried anything with me before?"

"You're my sister's best friend. You're a seventeen-year-old kid."

Blinding anger exploded in her. She seized the front of his jacket and jerked it. "I'm not a kid, Michael," she said through gritted teeth. "Stop treating me like I'm some stupid kid."

Michael gathered her clenched fists in his hands and locked her eyes with his. His gaze stung and she felt naked and hot all over. His voice came low, his words gentle. "You're right, Jory. You're no kid. You're pretty and soft and very much a woman. You don't deserve to have it happen for you this way."

Michael was rejecting her! The realization jolted Jory, and her anger became burning humiliation. She averted her eyes and mumbled, "You were drunk and I was scared because of almost having an accident. We got carried away talking about Melissa and . . . and . . ." She struggled to rise, to get out of the car and run off. "We were just two c-crazy people . . ." Her voice wavered.

Michael hauled her back down. "If this had happened to Melissa and I found out about it, I would have gone after the guy with my bare hands."

He sounded as if he were apologizing to her, but her head was beginning to throb and she couldn't sort things out. "You don't have to make up excuses, Michael. I'm a big girl."

"Jory, listen to me." His tone pleaded and he held her hands so tightly that it hurt. "I can't even help myself. I don't know up from down, right from left. But I do know what's right and wrong, and this, with you, out here in the woods, in the backseat of your car, is wrong. I should never have come here alone with you."

"I'll take you back to the party." Her tone was wooden and she felt as stiff as a tree. "You can get your truck and leave."

"I don't have my keys."

She reached into the pocket of her sweatshirt and pulled out his ring of keys. "I have them." He looked startled. She explained, "You were too drunk to drive. I thought I was doing you a favor."

He took them, letting his fingers linger on hers. "You were right. Thanks."

"My good deed for the night," she retorted and climbed into the front seat, still drowning in shame and unwilling to look Michael in the eye. They drove in silence, and at the party site he got out. He hesitated but she didn't allow him to speak. She threw the car into reverse and the tires spit gravel and dirt as she pulled away.

Jory made it home and quietly let herself into the sprawling, sleeping house. In her room, she undressed quickly and slipped between fresh, cool sheets. She stared into the darkness, numb and empty. She wanted to cry, but now the tears, which had threatened all the way home, refused to come.

Jory shivered and curled herself into a ball. She wished she had someone to talk to. Someone to tell about what had happened between her and Michael and help her understand. She couldn't tell her mother. The notion caused a sardonic smile. She couldn't tell Melissa, because Melissa was sick. And even if she weren't, how could Jory tell her about something so personal between herself and Melissa's own brother?

Lyle. She could tell Lyle. Not really, of course, but somehow she knew that deep down he would understand and help her make sense of it. "You must have a screw loose, Jory," she muttered. She'd been mean and hateful to Lyle and had all but told him to get lost. He'd never want to talk to her again. Michael had been right for years in his assessment of her. She was nothing more than a silly, ditzy girl. A kid.

The phone rudely woke Jory the next morning. At first, she tried to ignore it, burying her head under her pillow, but the thing refused to be quiet.

She gave up, groped for the receiver, and mumbled sleepily, "Hello."

"Jory, it's Michael."

She was instantly awake. "Yes?"

"Melissa's better, Jory. She's done a one hundred and eighty degree turn. Her white blood count is over four thousand, her platelets are up around fifty thousand, and her hemoglobin is ten point six."

"That's good?" Jory asked, trying to clear her head.

"It's terrific. It means that my bone marrow is doing the job, Jory. It's working."

Chapter Fifteen

Since it was a Sunday, the highway wasn't crowded and Jory made it to the hospital in record time. She hurried through the isolation ward and almost flattened Mrs. Austin, who was just leaving Melissa's room. "Isn't it wonderful?" Melissa's mother asked, her eyes shining.

"Fabulous," Jory cried. "Can I see her?"

"She's been asking about you." Mrs. Austin pulled off her sterile gown and stuffed it into a special container by the door.

Jory paused and shifted from foot to foot. "Uh . . . where's Michael?"

"He had to go to work. Evidently, he took last night off and now has to make it up. He looked like the devil this morning too," Mrs. Austin added, almost to herself.

Jory was relieved that she didn't have to face him first thing this morning. Not after what had happened the night before. "How is Melissa feeling?"

"By comparison, like a million dollars. The change is dramatic, Jory. Of course, the doctors say that she's still not out of the woods, but the latest results of her blood work are very encouraging."

Jory made a face. "Oh, those doctors would be pessimistic if we won the state lottery."

Mrs. Austin laughed. "You're right. Go on in, Jory, but don't stay too long. She thinks she's stronger than she actually is."

Jory put on the sterile scrubs, then pulled open a second door to Melissa's room. Her friend was sitting up in bed devouring breakfast, a plate heaped with scrambled eggs, grits, sausage, toast, and jelly. Jory watched, speechless.

Melissa smiled and waved between bites. "What's the matter? You've seen me eat before."

"Not that *fast*," Jory said. "And never anything that fast that wasn't drenched in chocolate."

"It's my blood that's messed up, Jory, not my stomach."

"I guess so."

Melissa shoved the plate aside. "Come here— give me a hug!"

Jory wrapped her arms around her friend. Melissa felt thin and feather light. "I've missed seeing you," Jory said, smiling to disguise her shock.

Melissa patted her bed. "So sit down and tell me all the news from school. What's happening?"

Jory took a chair and pulled in close to the bed. Where should she begin? How could she catch someone up on six weeks of life? "We had a carnival at school for you." She quickly filled Melissa in on the details.

"You mean people came and gave blood and donated money for me?" Melissa asked. "That means so much, Jory. It really does. I didn't realize that so many people really care. I know Mom can use the money too. I think her insurance ran out long ago."

Jory couldn't imagine what it would be like to worry about paying a bill. "We had a good time, and besides—you know me—any excuse for a party."

"Who helped?"

"The whole school. Especially the senior class."

"But you were the instigator?"

"Well, me and Lyle Vargas."

Melissa looked surprised. "Lyle?"

"He . . . um . . . he's been pretty nice . . ."

"But you don't like him? As a boyfriend, I mean."

"No way," Jory said. "We worked together, that's all. There's nothing going on with us, and I'm not looking for anything to be going on either."

"Are you still hung up on Michael?"

Jory suddenly felt extremely warm. "Haven't I always been?" She couldn't deny that she was still attracted to him, regardless of the fact that he'd rejected her the night before. "Some things will never change, Melissa. But I'm trying not to let it cramp my style." Jory didn't ever want Melissa to know how frustrated she felt about Michael.

Melissa plucked at the covers. "Tell me everything about school. And I mean *everything*. I even want to know what they've served in the lunchroom since I've been gone."

Jory began to relate everyday occurrences, silly

gossip, who was dating whom. Even the tiniest, most boring details made Melissa smile, and Jory wished she'd been more observant so she'd have more to tell.

"Any word on National Merit finalists yet?" Melissa asked.

"You told me they won't be announced until April," Jory reminded her.

"I know. I'm just getting antsy now that I feel better. It seems like I've been here a year and life is passing me by. All I want is to go home."

"When do you think they'll let you out?"

Melissa shrugged. "No one answers a direct question like that around here. They keep telling me it's too soon to tell. There's also been some more damage to my heart."

Jory felt her stomach plummet as if she were on an elevator falling too fast. "How much damage?"

"They'll do another EKG in the morning. It should give the cardiac specialist a better idea."

The ordeal isn't over yet, thought Jory. She wondered if Michael knew. "I sure hope this specialist gets you in top shape soon, Melissa. You've got to get out of this place—we've got a zillion plans to make for the prom."

"The prom?" Melissa studied Jory as if she'd suddenly grown another head.

"You know, the senior prom. The once-in-a-lifetime event every senior girl lives and breathes for."

"Jory, who's going to take *me* to the prom?"

"We don't know yet, now do we? But somebody will."

Melissa reached out and took Jory's wrist. "Don't you dare set something up, Jory. Don't you bribe some poor kid and beg him to take me."

"I wouldn't do that," Jory exclaimed, secretly calculating whom she could approach. "I think we should double-date, that's all. Cripes, Melissa, no one's even asked *me* yet."

Melissa interrupted, her voice pleading. "Jory, please listen to me. You can't manage my life this way."

"I don't do that!"

"The heck you don't," Melissa countered. "Maybe the prom is like the Brain Bowl for me this year—something I can't go to. I don't want to even think about the prom right now. Or where I'm supposed to get the money for a new dress. Besides, I've seen myself in the mirror and I look like a circus freak . . ."

Jory hadn't meant to upset Melissa. She'd only wanted to give her something to look forward to. "Okay. We won't talk about the prom now. We'll have lots of time for that later." She rose to her feet, patting Melissa's hand and saying, "You get some rest and I'll come back tomorrow. And call me if you want anything."

Tired, Melissa sank slowly down under the covers. "You get too involved, Jory."

"No I don't. I'm just looking to the future. After all, you'll be away at college this time next year and won't be home until summer vacation.

We'd better have all the fun we can before we leave Lincoln High."

Melissa sighed. "I'm sure you won't let me leave without a ticker tape parade either. Did you ever stop to think that I may not want to come back here?"

Jory grinned, dismissing her comment with a wave. "Goodbye doesn't have to mean *forever*, Melissa. I want to make it worth your while to come back, that's all." Jory promised to return later, and she went into the air lock, where she stood for a few minutes against the door, trying to calm her racing pulse and catch her breath.

Jory parked her car at the far back corner of the Steak 'n Shake restaurant after school. She ordered fries and a cola from the curb service waitress and scrunched down in the seat, hoping no one from school would see her. Right now she wanted to be alone.

Her latest run-in with her mother still thundered through her head. Mrs. Delaney had confronted Jory the minute she had gotten home from school, brandishing Jory's most recent grade sheet under her nose.

"What have you got to say about *these*, young lady?"

Jory shrugged and waved the computer printout aside. "I'm not a scholar."

"Look at this!" Her mother continued. "Cs, a D, and even an Incomplete. How do you ever expect to get accepted to the University of Miami with grades like this?"

"You're the one who wants me to go to the U of M, Mother. I never said I wanted to go there."

"Well don't worry. With these grades, you couldn't get into a vocational school! What is the matter with you, Jory? Where is your common sense? *Everybody* goes to college. You can't expect to make it in the world without a degree."

Jory silently counted to ten, then dropped her books on the spotless kitchen counter with a thud. "Stop pushing me. Stop forcing me to decide about college right now. I've got a zillion things on my mind, Mom, and getting into the U of M is at the bottom of the list."

"Jory, I haven't said much about the inordinate amount of time you spend dealing with Melissa . . ."

"She's sick, Mother. I can't abandon her."

"I'm not asking you to, but for heaven's sake, keep it in perspective. You act like you're one of *her* family instead of *ours*. You're not, Jory."

Jory felt as if her mother had slapped her. She was about to say something angry and cutting when the phone rang. Mrs. Delaney grabbed the receiver, listened for a moment, and snapped, "Can't you handle it, Lucille?" Jory leaned back on the counter. "Oh, all right," Mrs. Delaney grumbled. "I'll be there in fifteen minutes." She hung up and turned toward Jory. "I have to go to the office. But don't think that this discussion is finished, young lady. It isn't—not by a long shot."

Jory watched her mother sweep out the door and felt hollow and numb. She picked up the crumbled grade sheet, glanced over it, and was forced to admit that her grades were pretty bad. She really didn't know why she hadn't tried harder. According to her SAT scores, she was smart enough to have done better.

She tossed the paper onto the counter. She glanced around the kitchen at the gleaming appliances and the freshly scrubbed counters and sinks, smelling of disinfectant and lemon wax. Mrs. Garcia had the place sparkling. *As clean and sterile as Melissa's hospital room*, Jory thought.

"Here's your order, honey." The waitress's voice snapped Jory out of her funk. She paid for the food and nibbled halfheartedly on the fries. They weren't greasy enough. Jory gazed out the window. Across the parking lot she recognized a car full of guys from school. She saw Lyle in the front seat, and he was staring straight into her eyes.

Jory almost smiled at him, but she remembered what he'd told her about flashing smiles she really didn't mean. Her face felt frozen. Flustered, Jory looked away.

When she looked up again, the boys had gone inside the restaurant and the car was empty.

Chapter Sixteen

"What do you mean Melissa has another fever? I just saw her two days ago and she was perfectly fine." Jory had met Mrs. Austin at the hospital.

Mrs. Austin rubbed her eyes, and Jory saw the exhaustion in her face. "Well, she's not perfectly fine now. She's spiking a fever and the lab people are running around like mad."

Jory swallowed hard. "Is it . . . I mean, could she be rejecting the transplant?"

"No. They're certain that the transplant is taking hold. Her white blood cell and platelet counts keep climbing. It's something else entirely. Dr. Rowan's called in another specialist."

"Gee, Mrs. Austin, I'm really sorry."

"So am I, Jory. I don't think I can take much more of this. First they give you hope, then it's snatched away. Then hope again, followed by despair. My nerves are shot."

Melissa's mother looked frazzled and Jory wanted to reach out to her, but didn't know if it would be proper. "Maybe I'll come back later," Jory said, not wanting to leave, but not sure she should stay.

"No," Mrs. Austin said, taking Jory's arm.

"Don't go yet. Melissa's asked to see you. The doctors don't want visitors except the immediate family, but Melissa's begged me to let you come in."

"I . . . uh . . . I think of Melissa as my sister," Jory said softly, shifting from foot to foot because the sense of urgency was scaring her.

Mrs. Austin nodded. "So does Melissa, Jory. And so do I."

"Can I go in right now?"

"Michael's in there with her, but go on anyway. If anyone says anything to you, send them to me."

Jory struggled into the sterile gown, finding it difficult to tie the strings on her mask because her fingers were shaking. She took a deep breath, swallowing the lump that had formed in her throat, and went into Melissa's room.

The room was crowded with even more machinery than Jory had seen before. Something ominous, with hoses and an oxygen tank, stood in a corner. Jory ignored it and turned her attention toward the bed, where Michael sat holding his sister's hand. He looked up as Jory entered and from over the top of his mask Jory felt his searing blue eyes burn holes right through her.

Cautiously, Jory approached the bed. Melissa's breathing was light and shallow. Her cheeks were flushed and her skin appeared translucent. "H-How is she?"

"Not so good." Michael's voice was brusque and Jory got the impression that he resented her intrusion.

"Your mother said for me to come in," she explained apologetically.

"The fever's wringing her out. She's in and out, so don't expect too long a social call."

His words were like tiny barbs and Jory winced. What had she done to make him dislike her so? The night in the car had been like a time warp, when the rules of life had been suspended and they'd reached out and joined with one another in some special way. Now, here in Melissa's room, it was as if that night had never happened. "Can I touch her?"

"Sure," Michael said grudgingly.

Jory stroked Melissa's forehead. It was dry and hot. She watched the rapid rise and fall of Melissa's chest through the thin material of her gown and followed the wire leads taped inside the material to the monitor where the green line zipped, fast and ragged. "She doesn't look good."

"Tell me about it."

Jory blushed, feeling stupid for making such inane comments. "What do they think is wrong?"

"They haven't said."

"But it isn't rejection?"

"No. My bone marrow's working just fine. Ironic, huh? The cure works, but the patient's still sick."

"Sh-She'll be all right. They'll find out what's got her and give her medicine, and she'll be all right again."

Melissa's eyelids fluttered open. "Hi, Melissa,"

Jory said gently, managing a smile. "It's only me. I stopped by to see if you'd like me to bring you a chocolate cheesecake or something."

Melissa slowly focused on Jory's face. "Maybe some other time. Are you skipping school?"

"Me? Come on, you know I never skip school. Why, I hear I'm up for the perfect attendance award this year."

"You've got to get serious about your life, Jory. You have so many things to do . . ." Melissa sounded almost pleading, ignoring Jory's attempt at humor. "You've got to go do them. You've got to do *everything*." Melissa realized that Michael was holding her hand and softened her grave expression. "Hi, Big Brother. You look like a doctor."

"No need to insult me, Sis." He squeezed her fingers. "How are you feeling?"

"Like a train ran over me. Do they know what's wrong?"

"Not yet. But you'll probably shrug it off before they figure it out."

Jory added, "Yeah. After all, you've got all that good bone marrow now."

"I'm so tired," Melissa said with a sigh that made Jory's heart skip a beat.

"Would you like us to leave so that you can sleep?" Michael asked.

"Oh no, don't leave. Please. I don't want to be alone. I want you—all of you—with me. Where's Mom?"

"Probably tearing some unsuspecting doctor

apart." Michael stroked Melissa's cheek. "I won't leave you."

Melissa turned toward Jory. "I thought it would hurt, but it doesn't."

Jory wondered what Melissa meant by *it*. She didn't ask, but she didn't like the way Melissa was talking. She sounded weary and resigned. "They'll give you shots for pain if you hurt, won't they?" Jory asked.

"They give me shots. I've had a bunch of shots. But every time I wake up, it's nice to have one of you with me. I like knowing I'm not by myself, and that I'm not facing this alone."

Jory exchanged quick glances with Michael. "Well, here we are," she said brightly.

"I'm acting like a baby, aren't I?" Jory and Michael shook their heads in unison. "Yes, I am," Melissa said. "I don't know why I'm acting so weird. It's just that I'm lonely and so tired. I think I could sleep for a month, but I'm sort of afraid too."

"How so?" Michael asked.

"What if I don't wake up?"

A sudden chill shook Jory. Why was the air-conditioning on? Didn't the hospital realize that Melissa's room felt like a meat locker?

"I'll shake you until you do wake up," Michael said.

"You shouldn't hold on so hard, Michael."

He dropped her hand. "Gosh, I'm sorry. Was I hurting your hand?"

Melissa smiled in a strange way. "I didn't mean my hand," she said.

Jory's teeth began to chatter. She felt her breath growing short and wondered if she might be catching a cold. It wouldn't do to be around Melissa if she was catching something. "Look, maybe I should be going."

Melissa glanced back at her. "I want you to take the journal," she said.

Jory's mouth opened, then closed. She wanted to cry, "No!" Instead she asked, "Really? Right now? What if I lose it? What if I can't think of anything to write? What if . . .?"

Melissa tapped Jory's hand. "You promised."

"But I can bring it back just as soon as you're feeling better, right?"

"Sure."

Michael eyed her stonily as Jory reached into the bedside table drawer and removed the blue leather book. Jory hugged it to her chest, staring only at Melissa and trying desperately not to allow Michael's hostile eyes into her line of vision. "I promised your mother that I wouldn't stay long. I'll track her down and tell her you want to see her. That way Michael won't have to leave."

Melissa managed a half wave. "Come see me again soon, Jory, and don't forget to keep up the journal."

Jory made it out of the room and into the corridor, where she leaned against a wall and struggled to catch her breath. She felt as if she'd run ten miles. She found Mrs. Austin and quickly left the hospital. In the parking lot, she sat in her car with the top down, resting her head on the seat and staring at the brilliant blue sky and white glowing sun until her eyes hurt. She wished the noonday sun would warm her.

The party seemed endless. Franklin Cortez, the last of Mrs. Delaney's prearranged dates for Jory, was trying hard to be charming, but Jory had no interest in him or in the party.

Jory watched her parents dancing. Her father was tall and bronzed by the sun. His silver hair gave him a distinguished look. Her mother was elegant, almost regal-looking in a flowing chiffon gown. They were a perfect couple glowing with good looks and good health. Jory wished she were at the hospital with the Austins.

"Melissa has meningitis." Jory would never forget the sound of Mrs. Austin's words as long as she lived. The diagnosis had come four days before, striking like a hammer blow. Meningitis. The membranes surrounding Melissa's brain and spinal cord were inflamed. She wasn't responding to treatment and her heart was damaged and very weak.

Jory hadn't seen Melissa since the day her friend had insisted she take the journal. The book weighed on Jory's conscience. She hadn't touched it since she'd taken it home and hidden it away in a drawer in her room for safekeeping. It was Melissa's and full of her private thoughts. For Jory to read it or write in it wouldn't be right. It seemed like eavesdropping to her.

Franklin interrupted her thoughts by saying he liked her dress. Jory thanked him. It *was* a beautiful dress, emerald green, strapless, with a flared skirt that came just above her knees. Jory's mother had outdone herself in choosing it, for it complemented her auburn hair perfectly. But right now, Jory couldn't have cared less. She felt an urge to escape. To escape Franklin and the party and an incredible sense of sadness.

She excused herself, smiling gaily at Franklin and promising to be right back. Instead, she went to the front entrance and, without a second thought, left the club and drove off in her car. She wanted to be alone. She needed time to think.

It was after one A.M. when she turned into her driveway. She was surprised to see all the lights still on. She groaned. That meant her mother was waiting for her, and Jory knew she'd be on the warpath. After all, Jory had simply walked out of the country club without telling her parents or Franklin Cortez that she was going. How could she explain herself? How could she make her mother understand that she couldn't have stayed there one more minute without screaming? Jory sighed, squared her shoulders, and walked quickly into the house.

"Where have you been?" Her mother stood alone in the living room, her arms crossed.

"Driving."

"Since nine o'clock?"

"Yes." Jory put her keys in her purse, snapped it shut, and dropped it onto the cherry wood end table. "Listen, Mother, I know I shouldn't have run off, but I was bored stiff. I know you're mad, but I'm really wiped out. Could we have our fight about it in the morning?"

"Jory, I need to tell you something."

Jory's gaze flew to her mother's face. She expected anger and fire. She saw wariness and . . . tears? Jory stiffened and said, "Not tonight, Mother. I'm exhausted. I'll get up early and we can talk then."

Mrs. Delaney stepped in front of Jory as she started to leave. "Mrs. Austin called here about ten tonight, and Mrs. Garcia called us at the club."

Jory felt her heart pounding. "Tell me in the morning," she said, trying to step around her mother.

"Jory, you must listen to me."

"I don't want to listen." Jory fought a rising sense of panic. The walls seemed to be closing in. Why wouldn't her mother get out of her way? Childlike, Jory clamped her hands over her ears. "I can't hear you, Mother. I'm not going to listen."

Mrs. Delaney reached out, took Jory's wrists, and tugged. "Melissa died tonight, honey. Her heart gave out."

Jory felt her throat constrict. She stared wide-eyed because the awful words confirmed what she'd known deep inside, all along. What she'd realized the moment Mrs. Austin had told her about Melissa's meningitis. "I-I'll go to bed now and get some sleep. I'll . . . um . . . call Mrs. Austin tomorrow. She must be hurting. And Michael too. He wasn't prepared for this, you know. He wasn't ready for it . . ."

Mrs. Delaney gently shushed Jory's senseless babbling, smoothing her palm over Jory's hair and down her cheek. "I'm so sorry, baby. So sorry."

"Don't leave me alone."

"I won't, Jory. I'm right here. For as long as you want."

Without warning, a wail started deep within Jory's soul and rose, until it ripped its way out her mouth. Her whole body began to tremble and she would have crumbled, except that her mother wrapped her arms around her and supported her. Mrs. Delaney stroked Jory's hair and crooned nonsensical things, as a mother would to a child, rocking her, comforting her, while Jory wept for hours into the night.

Chapter Seventeen

Melissa Austin was buried on a glorious day in March that looked like a greeting card colored in bright crayons. The sky gleamed sapphire blue and the sun was a fiery yellow. The breeze smelled of flowers and new grass. Lincoln High School closed at noon and the senior class, and even some juniors and sophomores, came to bury their classmate, who, according to the student newspaper, had "died too young."

The cortege of automobiles wound its way through the streets of Tampa in a slow, steady crawl to the cemetery. Jory inched along in the snaking line, alone in her convertible. Her parents had driven too, and they were somewhere behind in traffic. It meant a lot to her that they had come. But she'd driven by herself because despite her mother's kindness and understanding, today she could not share her grief with anyone.

Jory surmised that grief had an anesthetic quality to it. She had functioned in a normal capacity during the few days following Melissa's death, without remembering exactly how she'd made it through. She'd eaten and slept, and talked to her parents and made phone calls to friends. But she'd felt numb, detached, as if she were moving through mist in a dream.

Now she had time to think, and the previous days came back in bits and pieces. She recalled weeping with Mrs. Austin in the kitchen, the friendly yellow kitchen she'd all but grown up in since fifth grade.

"She doesn't hurt anymore," Mrs. Austin said. "In some ways, knowing that makes it easier for me."

Jory wanted to shout, "It's a lousy price to pay to never hurt again," but instead she plucked at a tissue in her fist and said, "Melissa was the bravest person I ever knew."

"It's hard to believe she'll never come through that door again."

"I know."

"That she'll never call me up and ask, 'Mom, what do you want me to start for supper?'"

"I know," Jory said, and she and Mrs. Austin held each other and cried.

Later, Jory had gone to Melissa's bedroom, but she lost her courage and shut the door quickly, staring at it so long that her knees locked. She had avoided Michael, who looked to have aged ten years. He wore dark glasses, even inside the house, and he never once spoke to her until the day of the viewing at the funeral home.

Jory had been the first one there aside from the immediate family, but she couldn't bring herself to walk over to the open casket. The notion of seeing Melissa's body terrified her, yet she knew she couldn't leave without telling her best friend good-bye.

Struggling to keep her composure, Jory watched Michael approach the coffin and, as he knelt down her courage returned. Timidly she went forward and knelt next to him. Her hands were clammy and her throat ached with unshed tears, but she forced herself to look at Melissa who rested on a bed of white satin. "Crazy, isn't it?" Michael said. "She had to die in order to be beautiful again."

Jory nodded, awestruck. Melissa *was* beautiful, dressed in white eyelet, her hair—the wig Jory had given her—framing her flawless face. She was no longer bloated, and the sores and lesions were smoothed away. Jory said, "Death gave her back what life took away. She looks like a princess." Then she asked Michael, "Does your father know? Was there any way to let him know?"

Michael's eyes never strayed from his sister's face. "He left years ago and if Mom has an address for him, she never told me. But I wouldn't want him here. Why should he share her death, when he never shared her life?"

Jory allowed herself one final lingering look at her friend, then she stepped aside and watched others file past. Ric came. She recognized his sharp features and shaggy brown hair immediately. He was with a girl Jory didn't know. Michael's friends came too. People she recognized from the balloon club, and the guy who'd asked Jory to drive Michael home on the night of the party in the woods.

Kids from school came. Jory caught snatches of their conversations.

"It's awful, so awful."

"Poor Melissa. Why did this have to happen to her?"

"She had everything to live for. It's not fair."

"I thought she was getting better, then just after Christmas, bam! Back to the hospital."

"I'm glad I gave blood. It makes me feel I helped in some small way."

Many of the girls wept and for some reason it irritated Jory, for they hadn't known Melissa half as well as she, and she was taking great pride in staying dry-eyed throughout the evening. She refused to cry in front of them. Melissa would have wanted her to keep it together, because Jory had a reputation for smiling, for always having a happy-go-lucky attitude. It was the least she could do for Melissa. The very least.

Lyle came, of course. She saw him across the room, walking past the casket, tall and lean, his amber eyes downcast and serious. He was dressed in a dark brown suit and there were streaks of blond in his hair from being outdoors a lot.

Lyle stepped away and glanced up. Jory tried to look down to avoid meeting his eyes, but she was too late. Lyle nodded, acknowledging her, and their estrangement reared between them like a wall. She had avoided him for weeks, ever since the night of the party when they'd fought. She turned quickly to scan the masses of funeral bouquets. Seeing him had suddenly made her throat tighten and tears threaten. Jory clenched her teeth, dug her nails into her palms. *This is stupid*, she told herself. How could she make it through this terrible evening without shedding a tear, then almost lose it because she'd looked into Lyle Vargas's eyes? It made no sense.

She had slipped away right after seeing Lyle and gone home. Now, as the endless line of cars filed through the gates of the cemetery, Jory remembered how confused she'd felt that night of the viewing. And she couldn't call Melissa and ask, "What's the matter with me? Why am I acting so dopey?"

The graveside area was crowded with people overflowing from under a canvas canopy, where a minister waited and Melissa's few relatives sat stiffly in chairs. Michael wore a black suit and dark glasses. His expression was stony and he held his mother's hand without moving. Jory's heart ached. The minister spoke of heaven and how Melissa was already there. Jory glanced away, toward the section of the cemetery where she'd brought Melissa last winter to see Rachael's grave. She wondered if Melissa was playing with the little girl.

The minister read some Bible verses. Jory tried to concentrate on the words but couldn't. He said, "And I will turn your mourning into joy," and the idea was so ludicrous to Jory that she almost laughed out loud. The minister's voice seemed to be coming from far away and Jory felt a lightness in her head. Her vision blurred and the ground tilted.

She felt an arm around her waist as she sagged.

Her legs collapsed, beyond her control. A guy's voice said, "Come with me. You'd better sit down."

She allowed him to lead her away from the service toward the line of parked cars. Her breath was coming in short gasps and she felt sick to her stomach, cold and clammy. A car door opened and hands guided her into the cool interior of a large gray automobile. "Lean back against the seat," his voice said.

Shakily, she obeyed, but her breathing was erratic. "W-why can't . . . I catch . . . my . . . breath?"

"You're hyperventilating. Put your head between your knees. Your brain needs oxygen. Relax." He dipped her head forward, all the while holding her hand. "You almost fainted. You were as white as a sheet, but your color's better already."

Jory did as she was told. In a few minutes, her head began to clear and her breathing slowed. She sat up and confronted her white knight. *Lyle*. Words of thanks died on her lips as Jory felt extreme embarrassment. "I think I'm all right now," she mumbled. "I need to get back. I'm missing the service."

Lyle held her shoulder gently, restraining her. "Not so fast, or it'll happen all over again."

Jory felt woozy and realized he was right. She dropped back onto the car seat and closed her eyes. The car was cool and quiet, and she welcomed the relief from the sun. She kept her eyes closed, still embarrassed. Finally, she said, "Thanks for the rescue."

Lyle explained, "I happened to glance over and you looked so pale I thought, 'Jory's going down.' So I moved next to you as fast as I could. I don't think too many people noticed."

She hoped not. Jory felt utterly ridiculous and foolish. "I've never fainted in my life."

"You've been under a lot of stress. Sometimes it comes out in odd ways and at inconvenient times."

"You'll make a great doctor, Lyle." It came out sarcastically and she saw him flinch.

He gazed out the car window. "The service is over."

An incredible sadness filled Jory. "I missed the minister's final words." Her tone was flat. "About how happy we'll all be someday."

"Come on," Lyle said. "I'll take you to your car."

She let him help her out because her legs were still wobbly. She leaned on the car door. "I can make it," she told him.

"You shouldn't drive."

"I can drive fine. Stop treating me like an invalid."

"Are you all right, Jory?" It was Michael.

Instinctively, she leaned toward him. "I'm all right," she said. Lyle's eyes darted between Michael and Jory. He stepped aside.

"Mom saw you almost faint and she was worried."

"Lyle rescued me."

Lyle and Michael exchanged nods. Michael

adjusted his dark glasses. "Mom wants you to come back to the house for the afternoon. Everybody on the block sent food and we have enough for all the relatives and their relatives too."

Jory agreed. She wanted to be with the Austins. It made Melissa seem closer, more tangible. "I'll be there soon. Let me tell my parents."

Michael walked away and Lyle turned his attention to Jory. "If you ever want to talk, Jory, call me."

"I don't want to talk. All I want to do is forget."

"Well, you take care. I'll . . . uh . . . see you next week in school."

Jory looked at him, and a deep, dark despair welled inside her, making her throat ache. "Melissa would have been eighteen years old next month. We were planning to go register to vote."

"Goodbye, Jory," Lyle said.

She watched him, unblinking, as he walked away. She gripped her arms tightly to her chest and allowed her gaze to drift to the canopy and to the coffin waiting to be lowered into the ground. Baskets of flowers and wreaths stood vigil around the pale blue casket and spilled over in lush abundance, reminding Jory more of a garden than of a funeral. Their colorful, velvet petals fluttered in the breeze—jonquils and daffodils, daisies and iris, pansies, black-eyed Susans, tulips, lilies, and exotic birds of paradise. "A thousand pretty petals," Jory said under her breath. "With nothing to do but die."

Chapter Eighteen

~

February 19

Dear Jory,

If you're reading this, it means you finally picked up my journal and found this letter I stuck in the back for your eyes only. It also means that I have probably died, because that's the only way you would have picked up the book in the first place. Sorry—just a bit of dark humor.

It's three o'clock in the morning here in the hospital and all I have is the beep from my monitor to keep me company. They say the transplant is working, but they still won't let me out of here. If I regret anything, it's that I had to spend my last days trapped in this place, when I'd rather have been at home. Anyway, I wanted to get this written while I'm lucid and sane (no smart aleck cracks, Jory!).

I know they say I'm getting better, but I don't think I believe them. I'm not giving up, but I'm not clinging to false hope either. You know, it's not death that's so hard—it's getting there. Sort of like waiting in the dentist's office, knowing some horrible torture waits, only to think once it's over, "That wasn't so bad."

If I am dead when you read this, I hope that you're not all sad and weepy over me. Oh, I expect you to cry, but please don't get carried away. There's too much for you to see and do instead of crying over me. Go to the prom. Okay? And wear your cap and gown to graduation no matter how dorky you feel in it. I would have graduated, so make sure Mom gets my diploma and my tassel.

Kids don't make out wills, Jory. But I do have a few worldly possessions that I want you to have. Mom knows, because I've written her and Michael letters too. You get the program from the Springsteen concert. You got the autograph—and almost got trampled getting it—but you made me take the program. I want you to have it back. Also, keep the page from the coloring book little Rachael gave to me. I don't know why I've grown so attached to it, but I have. Maybe I understand what Cinderella must have felt like when she was having such a good time at the ball and heard the clock strike. She wasn't ready to leave, but knew she had to.

Of course, if there's any of my clothes you want, take them. And my barrette and combs collection. I haven't worn any of them since I lost my hair, but I couldn't bring myself to throw them away. Oh, take that stupid vase I made in seventh grade crafts, the one I accidentally recorded my thumbprint on before it was fired in the kiln.

Now to the serious stuff. Everyone's going to say, "How sad that Melissa died so young." I agree. There's a thousand things I'll never get to do. I'll never graduate from college, have a career, get married, have a baby (back up! I forgot "have sex"), watch my kids grow up, sit on the Supreme Court bench, and grow old with my husband. I was really mad about all that for a long time. I wanted all those things, and it stinks—really stinks—that I have terminal cancer instead.

But Jory, I've had lots of time to lie here and think this out. There were plenty of things I did get to do. I saw the sun rise and set over six thousand times, I petted fuzzy little kittens and puppies, tasted chocolate, smelled roses and gardenias, and heard the ocean in a seashell. I kissed Brad Kessing, and Ric kissed me and made me feel all gooey inside and at least invited me to go to bed with him—which I was real tempted to do. Sometimes I wish I had, but other times I'm glad I didn't. This way, they can bury me in virginal *white with a clear conscience. Sorry, Jory, that's that black humor again. Keep remembering as you're reading this, it's three A.M. and Melissa is bored and alone, and trying to cram everything that's inside her into a few pages of a letter.*

I want to clear another thing up with you too. I'm not mad at God anymore, like I was that night on the beach. I've had some heart-to-heart talks with Him and I've come to believe that He loves me enough to want me with Him in heaven. And that once I'm in heaven, I'll never have to die again. (Just think. I get to do something before you do, Jory Delaney!) We all didn't come into the world at the same time, so it makes sense that we all won't leave it at the same time.

You once told me, "Goodbye doesn't mean forever." You're absolutely right. I know I'll see you and Mom and Michael again someday. I know I will. But knowing still doesn't make leaving any easier. All of you will miss me. And you'll feel sad and that makes me sad.

Jory, I know you love Michael and have for years. I don't know how it will work out between you, but I hope that whatever the outcome is, you're happy. Don't forget to go do something with your life, no matter what happens between you and Michael. I've never known anybody like you, Jory. You have a million, zillion things going for you. You light up a room just by walking through the door, and people like you, really like you. And no matter what, you've always been my very best friend.

I guess I'm starting to ramble now and get mushy, so I'd better cut it off before my heart monitor sends out an alarm and the nurses come running. I think you know what I mean by all this stuff I've written.

Also, you don't really have to write anything in my journal, Jory. It's mine and it should start and stop in my handwriting. But please make sure to give it to Mom. I've written down a lot of things about my illness and my feelings about my illness in the book. Maybe the doctors can use it to help some other girl my age who gets cancer. Who knows?

Be good and have a wonderful life. Name one of your kids for me. And never forget me. Because as long as one person remembers you, you're never really gone. (Doesn't that sound deep?) One day, you'll be happy again, and so will Mom and Michael. Always keep in touch with each other. I'll be watching you! And when you least expect it, you'll hear me call you in the wind. I promise.

Love, your friend, your sister,
Melissa

Jory didn't know how long it took her to read Melissa's letter because tears kept filling her eyes. After she read it, she cried for a long time, then tucked it back inside the envelope and put it safely away in her drawer.

Jory stood before Lyle's front door, trying to muster the courage to ring the bell. "This is dumb," she told herself. "Why did you come?" She could have seen Lyle at school, but instead she'd gotten up early on Saturday morning, looked up his address in the phone directory, and driven over to his house. She couldn't even explain why.

His neighborhood was nice, with large ranch-style homes and clipped, manicured lawns. From the porch, Jory saw a wheelbarrow full of mulch and a lawn mower in one corner of the yard. It amazed her that everything around her could appear so tidy and neat, while inside she was feeling such turmoil.

"It's now or never, Jory," she muttered. She took a deep breath and pushed the bell. No one answered and she almost turned away when the door flew open. Lyle stood in the doorway wearing cutoffs and a tank top and a sweatband around his forehead. "Jory!"

"Is this a bad time?"

"No, it's not a bad time at all. It's a good time. I was just about to start on the lawn. Come in."

She followed him inside, glancing about rooms that were casual and homey, with a lived-in look of scattered pillows and a newspaper on the floor and a few coffee cups perched on end tables. He led her into a big, friendly kitchen painted yellow. Jory felt a sense of déjà vu.

"Sit down," Lyle said, pulling out a bar stool and shoving aside breakfast dishes on the counter. "Sorry the place is a mess, but Dad's out playing a few rounds of golf and Mom took my sisters to ballet class."

"I didn't know you had sisters." Jory realized there was a lot she didn't know about Lyle, and a lot she suddenly wanted to know about him.

"Yeah, eleven-year-old twins." He flashed a grin. "I call them Tweedledum and Tweedledee. It drives them crazy."

She looked around. The walls were covered with pictures and plaques and sprays of flowers. Papers, obviously schoolwork, were stuck to the refrigerator with tiny magnets. "Mom never throws anything away," Lyle said. "If I didn't hide my term papers, they'd be plastered all over the fridge too."

"I like it," Jory told him. "It looks like real people live here."

"Yeah. Well, after Mom was diagnosed, our whole family began to rethink its priorities. At the bottom of her list was kitchen floors you could eat off of. We do more as a family now too. We learned the hard way about what's really important, and the time we spend together tops the list."

An unexpected lump stuck in Jory's throat. "Could I have a drink?"

Lyle hit his forehead with his palm. "What's the matter with me? Sure. How about some root beer?"

"Sounds good." She watched him find a glass in the cupboard, fill it with ice, and pour a frothy head of root beer.

He set it in front of her and leaned forward on the counter, bracing himself on his elbows. "I'm really surprised to see you. I mean, you didn't say you might drop by at school. But I'm glad you came." Jory nodded, still unable to clear her throat enough to speak. "Uh . . . why did you come, Jory?"

A hundred things raced through her brain, and nothing made sense. She wanted to run out the door and drive off. She wanted to throw herself on the kitchen floor, kicking and screaming. She wanted to crawl out of her skin because she hurt inside so bad. She gripped the glass until her knuckles hurt, almost pasted a silly smile on her face, and slid off the stool saying, "No reason. Just thought I'd stop by and visit. It's been a while since I've visited friends, that's all."

Jory's face felt stiff and frozen, and she wanted to cry. "You said if I ever wanted to talk . . ." Her voice was so low that Lyle had to stand directly in front of her to hear her. She fell silent.

Lyle reached out and placed his hand on the nape of her neck and drew her gently to his chest. With her forehead on his chest, and his hand warm and soothing on her skin, she slowly relaxed and took a long, deep breath. He smelled of clean, fresh soap. She squeezed her eyes shut. "I . . . well, if you're not too busy . . . maybe we could talk right now. I'll understand if you're too busy. I know I stopped by uninvited . . ."

"Hey, it's okay. I've got time." His fingers played with her hair. "Believe me, Jory, I've got all the time in the world for you."

Chapter Nineteen

~❧~

"Are you sure you're awake?" Michael asked Jory.

She stifled a yawn and wiggled into the corner of the cab of his truck. "I just forgot how early four o'clock in the morning comes. Want some coffee?"

He nodded and Jory poured him some from a thermos, being careful not to spill any as the truck moved along the dark, empty highway. She handed him the cup and cranked down the window. A muggy breeze flooded the cab. "It's going to be a long, hot summer," Jory observed. "It's only the middle of June and already I can feel the heat building for the day."

"You nervous?"

"About my first balloon ride?" She offered a wide smile. "Scared to death. What if I throw up?" The words evoked the memory of Melissa. Jory wished Melissa could have been with them. "You never told me why you wanted to take me up."

Michael sipped from the Styrofoam cup. "Melissa asked me to in a letter she left for me. It's just taken a while for me to get around to it. Do you mind?"

Jory understood. Michael would have done

anything for his sister. "It's been a busy time for all of us. What with graduation and all."

"It was nice of you to stop by dressed in your cap and gown. It meant a lot to Mom. Oh, and thanks for getting Melissa's diploma for us."

"No problem. She was a straight A student and made the dean's list—even if it was posthumously. She would have been pleased about the National Merit Scholarship too. I know how much she wanted it."

A line formed on Michael's mouth, as if the coffee had gone bitter. "I guess they gave it to someone else instead."

"A boy from Lincoln named Lyle Vargas. He's the guy who helped me on the day of the funeral when I almost fainted—do you remember him? Lyle wants to be a doctor." Jory smiled secretly. She'd been dating Lyle steadily since April. She remembered the night of the prom, when some of the gang had gone to the beach to watch the sun rise. Lyle had led her off alone. He'd rolled up the cuffs of his tuxedo, and they'd stood together in the moist sand with the cool water lapping over their bare feet, looking out over the dark, glassy sea. As dawn broke, Lyle had taken her in his arms, kissed her, and told her he loved her.

"So what are you going to do in the fall, Jory?"

She snapped back to reality. "Believe it or not, I'm going to college."

"I assumed you were," Michael said, puzzled.

"For a long time, I wasn't sure I even wanted to go. But after—you know—the funeral and all, well, I buckled down in school and suddenly I really wanted to work hard and go to college." She fidgeted with her hands. "Of course, I got a late start and my grades were pretty sorry, but I've been accepted at USF on academic probation. If I do well as a freshman, my parents said I could transfer to wherever I want to go."

Michael glanced over at her. "Any ideas where that might be?"

She thought of Lyle and how he'd been accepted at Duke. "Maybe someplace in North Carolina."

Michael turned the truck into a pasture and the ride turned bumpy. In the middle of the dark field, he stopped. Jory climbed out. A small group from the balloon club were already waiting, laying out their balloons and filling them with propane. "You want to help?" Michael asked.

"If I remember how," she said, scrambling to help him haul his balloon from the truck bed. They worked side by side without speaking. Jory stood back when the tank of propane was turned on for Michael's balloon. The nylon filled and rose lazily. Overhead, stars still twinkled although the horizon was turning gray.

When the balloon was filled and straining against its ropes, Michael offered Jory his hand. "Ready?"

Her heart thudded as she remembered all the times she'd longed to climb into the basket with him and sail off into the heavens. "Let's go," she said, taking his hand.

The basket rocked, and Jory gripped its edges as she found her footing. Michael adjusted the gas jets of the propane tank on board and called to the people holding the ropes, "Let her up!"

The ropes slackened and the balloon wobbled as they drifted upward. Jory watched the ground fall away, her heart in her throat. As the people and vehicles grew smaller, she felt a delightful floating sensation. "Oh, Michael! This is fabulous!"

She leaned out over the edge and Michael caught her arm. "Whoa! Not so far."

The balloon continued to rise, and Jory peered up at the sphere looming above. She wondered if she could reach out and pluck a star from the sky. "How high will we go?"

"Not too high. Things only get smaller the higher you go, and that's not half as interesting as just going up about a thousand feet and watching the world drift by."

She spotted the chase vehicle on the road below and it looked like a toy. Michael released a valve, and the balloon dipped toward a clump of trees. "What are you doing?"

"When we pass over the top of the trees, grab a leaf. It's good luck if you can snag one right off the top."

The basket skimmed the uppermost part of the trees. "This must be how a bird feels," she cried. How different a tree looked from the top. For the first time she was seeing the world from a unique perspective.

The basket brushed the treetops again. "Grab one!" Michael yelled.

Jory leaned out and the leaves fluttered, turning their soft undersides toward her. She felt as if they were clapping and she should take a bow. She snatched one from the very tip-top of the tallest tree and, laughing, clutched the fragile piece of green to her breast. "That was wonderful! Thank you, Michael."

He grinned boyishly, turned the jets higher, and the balloon once again soared upward. They floated, suspended between heaven and earth as the sky faded from indigo to gray-blue. "How long before the sun rises?"

"It's hard to say. You'll be drifting along and then suddenly, it's there. It's best if you can actually watch it pop over the horizon. But that's rare. Usually, it just turns from dawn into daylight."

Jory faced him across the compact basket, braced herself on the side of the gondola, and studied him. Wind ruffled his black hair and something stirred within her heart. When the blast from the gas died and only the soft hiss remained, she asked, "How have you been, Michael? How's it been going for you?"

He stared off to the horizon. "Some days are better than others. Sometimes I still can't believe she's really gone. It's like she's going to come through the door from school and throw her books on the table and yell at me for leaving the milk out or something." He dipped his head. "God, I miss her."

"I miss her too. Sometimes I think of something I want to tell her and I pick up the phone and get your number half dialed before I remember that she's not there."

"I'm still pretty mad about it," Michael confessed. "Why Melissa? Why her?"

Jory thought of what Melissa had written in the letter. *People will ask, Why Melissa?* She thought back to what Mrs. Austin had once told her, "*The rain falls on the just and the unjust.*" Jory rubbed her palm along the rim of the basket. "We may never know the answer to that, but I think Melissa found some answers for herself. I have a friend, Michael, a guy whose mother had cancer. She beat the odds and recovered, but he had the same sorts of questions. His whole family went through counseling and I've talked with him a lot over the past months, and he's helped me understand some things."

Michael glanced at her, but said nothing.

"I was angry about Melissa's being sick for a long time. I even denied it and told myself that she'd be all right. When she came out of remission and had to go back to the hospital, I got depressed—so depressed, in fact, that I had symptoms myself. My heart beat faster. My palms sweated. Whenever I even *thought* about Melissa's dying, I actually lost control of my own breathing. That's what happened to me on the day of the funeral. I stressed out." Jory shifted and the basket tilted with her. "And I felt guilty, Michael. I felt so bad because I was perfectly healthy, and she wasn't.

Yet I didn't want to take her place. And that made me feel more guilty. Maybe that's why I worked so hard on the blood drive. I was trying to make it up to her."

A small knowing smile crossed Michael's mouth. He folded his arms over his chest. "I know all about guilt. It was my bone marrow, remember? But then when it started working, I thought, 'All right! This is it. She's home free.' But she wasn't, was she?"

Jory heard the pain in his voice and wanted so much to touch him. She clung to the basket. Michael Michael tipped his head and asked, "Do you know that when she was sick the last time, I was actually mad at her for not getting well? I'd done my share. Why wasn't she doing hers? I thought she was giving up."

"I don't think she gave up. I think she just came to accept death. There's a difference between giving up and accepting. If we're going to get over Melissa's death, we have to accept it, too, the same way she did."

Michael sighed heavily. "I'm not there yet, Jory. I've still got a lot to work through."

Jory nodded. "Me too. But every day it's better for me," she added.

"I'm glad you've found some answers for yourself. In her letter to me, Melissa said that you 'loved life and people too much to let either get you down for long.'"

The way he quoted it brought a lump to Jory's throat. "She wrote me a great letter too, Michael. I'll treasure it for as long as I live."

"I told you in the truck, Jory, that I brought you up here because Melissa asked me to. But I also brought you for a reason of my own."

Her heart tripped and she smiled shyly. "To throw me over the side?"

He returned her smile. "I guess it must seem that way to you at times. I was never very nice and I've wanted to say I'm sorry for a long time."

Surprised, Jory straightened. "I know I've always been Melissa's pesky little rich friend to you, Michael. It's no secret."

"You shared things with her, Jory, that I couldn't share. I was only her brother, but you—well, you were her buddy. You two always seemed to have secrets, especially during her last visit to the hospital."

The notion that Michael had been jealous of their friendship stunned her. "Cripes, Michael, we were best friends and girls! Girls are like that. They just"—she hunted for the right words—"share things. But you were her brother and she worshipped the ground you walked on."

"You won't hold it against me?"

"I could never hold anything against you, Michael."

They stood staring at each other across the basket as it bobbed in the gathering morning light. Michael's face was awash in pink and gold, and his eyes had trapped the gold. Jory felt warm and content. She remembered the night she'd almost shared her body with him. Her feelings for Michael remained, but they had changed. She loved

Michael Austin, and a part of her would always love him. But Michael belonged to the sky, and to her childhood dreams.

Lyle, on the other hand, was like the earth— firm and solid and constant. Best of all, Lyle loved her, and she knew then, with the dawn inches from her fingertips, that she loved him too.

A gentle breeze blew, filling the basket and caressing Jory and Michael. It felt like silk against Jory's skin. "I feel like Melissa's here with us, Michael," she whispered.

"I know. I often feel like I'm in a cathedral when I'm up here. Like the earth's too small. Maybe that's why I came today and why I wanted you to come too. Maybe I thought the two of us together could touch her one more time."

Jory stepped next to him, and shoulder to shoulder they looked across the glowing heavens to where the curve of the horizon met the curve of the earth. The last clouds of night clung to the sky, then suddenly, the brilliant red-gold rim of the sun punched through them. Jory's breath caught at the sight and she felt an overwhelming sense of joy. She said, "We're going to make it, Michael. All of us are going to make it just fine."